**Hey, TodaysGirls! Check out 2day's
kewlest music, books, and stuff
when u hit *spiritgirl.com***

Published in Nashville, Tennessee, by Tommy Nelson®, a division of Thomas Nelson, Inc.

Scripture quotations are from the *International Children's Bible®, New Century Version®*: Copyright © 1986, 1988, 1999 by Tommy Nelson®, a division of Thomas Nelson, Inc.

Creative director: Robin Crouch
Storyline development & series continuity: Dandi Daley Mackall
Computer programming consultant: Lucinda C. Thurman

Library of Congress Cataloging-in-Publication Data
Kindig, Tess Eileen.
    Unpredictable / written by Tess Kindig / created by Terry K. Brown.
      p. cm. – (TodaysGirls.com ; 11)
    Summary: Because Bren feels she made a poor decision in the past, she finds it difficult to make choices on her own and turns to astrology for help.
    ISBN 0-8499-7714-2
    [1. Astrology—Fiction. 2. Choice—Fiction. 3. Agricultural exhibitions—Fiction. 4. Friendship—Fiction. 5. Christian life—Fiction.] I. Brown, Terry, 1961- II. Title. III. Series.

PZ7.K5663 Un 2001
[Fic]—dc21

                                       2001030544

Printed in the United States of America
01 02 03 04 05 PHX 9 8 7 6 5 4 3 2 1

UNPREDICTABLE

WRITTEN BY
Tess Kindig

CREATED BY
Terry K. Brown

Tommy nelson®
Thomas Nelson, Inc. • Nashville

Web Words

2 to/too

4 for

ACK! disgusted

AIMP always in my prayers

A/S/L age/sex/location

B4 before

BBL be back later

BBS be back soon

BD big deal

BF boyfriend

BFN bye for now

BRB be right back

BTW by the way

CU see you

Cuz because

CYAL8R see you later

Dunno don't know

Enuf enough

FWIW for what it's worth

FYI for your information

G2G or **GTG** I've got to go

GF girlfriend

GR8 great

H&K hug and kiss

IC I see

IN2 into

IRL in real life

JK just kidding

JLY Jesus loves you

JMO just my opinion

K okay

Kewl cool

KOTC kiss on the cheek

L8R later

LOL laugh out loud

LTNC long time no see

LY love you

NBD no big deal

NU new/knew

NW no way

OIC oh, I see

QT cutie

RO rock on

ROFL rolling on floor laughing

RU are you

SOL sooner or later

Splain explain

SWAK sealed with a kiss

SYS see you soon

Thanx (or) **thx** thanks

TNT till next time

TTFN ta ta for now

TTYL talk to you later

U you

U NO you know

UD you'd (you would)

UR your/you're/you are

WB welcome back

WBS write back soon

WTG way to go

Y why

(Note: Remember that capitalization may vary.)

chapter.1

"Tell me again why I'm here," Bren Mickler whined, following her best friend Jamie down an aisle of craft booths at the county fair. "There's not one thing in this whole place worth buying."

Jamie looked longingly at the horse barns in the distance. "I already told you. People don't go to the fair to shop," she explained. "The fair's about agriculture. Horses. Cattle. Goats. Produce. Pies. Canned succotash."

"Mmmmmm, goodie," Bren muttered, "lima beans." She fingered a pair of lumpy orange mittens for sale at the 4-H booth and shuddered.

"Well, it's your own fault Ms. Can't-Make-Up-Her-Mind. I asked you what you wanted to do today, and you couldn't decide, so I decided for you. Hey look—there's Maya on the Ferris wheel."

Bren shaded her almond eyes and gazed up at the giant revolving wheel on the midway. Maya Cross had wedged herself into a cart between two guys, one of whom could pass for Justin Timberlake. The girls waved, but Maya was too busy flirting to notice.

"Want to go see the horses?" Jamie asked when they failed to get Maya's attention. "You have to see the Clydesdales to believe them. They're huge. Even you'd be impressed."

Bren wrinkled her nose. "Horses smell. Anyway, it's too hot. Let's get some lemonade. Maybe they have the frozen kind. Tell me they at least have that."

"They have it," Jamie said. She took one last wistful look at the barns and headed for the green and yellow striped lemonade cart on the midway.

Bren dragged along behind her, strewing complaints like litter. "Look at my sandals. They're all covered with dust," she grumbled. Out of the six TodaysGirls, Bren and Maya were the most meticulous when it came to clothing. "I only have one pair of pink sandals, and now look at them. It's so hot, even my *head* is sweating. Dark colors soak up the sun like a sponge. So a person with dark hair gets much hotter than a person with light hair. That's a scientific fact. Oh noooooooooo!" She stopped dead in her tracks.

"You want large or small?" Jamie called. She'd reached the lemonade stand and was already in line.

"I just thought of something!" Bren wailed, running to catch up. "Jason Hersh called last week to ask me out, and I never got back to him."

"So call him when you get home. I think I'll have a small. You want a small too? Two small frozen lemonades," Jamie said to the woman operating the cart.

"Wait!" Bren tugged on Jamie's ponytail. "Maybe I want large," she protested. "No, I shouldn't. Too much sugar. But it must be 105 degrees out here. Maybe . . ."

"Two smalls," Jamie said firmly, pulling her ponytail away from Bren's reach. "They're on me." She paid for the lemonades and handed Bren a clear plastic cup mounded with yellow slush.

Bren took it and shrugged. "Thanks. I don't know what's the matter with me anymore. It's like I can't make a decision about anything. That's why I haven't called Jason. I can't decide whether I want him for a boyfriend or just a friend. If I say yes to this date, can you imagine the message I'd be sending? I already agreed to be his dance partner at youth group. They're making us learn square dancing this month. Ewwww!"

Jamie took a bite of frozen lemonade. "Hey, there's a row we missed," she said, pointing with the plastic spoon. "Let's go check it out, and then we'll try to find Maya."

Bren sighed and followed her friend past a booth selling goat's milk fudge. She'd rather watch nail polish dry than look at any more of this farmy stuff. "Did you hear what I said? Are you listening to me?" she demanded. "We're talking square dancing here. Locked together at the elbow while some hee haw yells, 'Swing Your Partner, Do-ri-tos!'"

"It's do-si-do. Not Doritos," Jamie said with a chuckle.

Bren rolled her eyes. Square dancing was not the point. The point was that she couldn't decide what to do about Jason. Just like she couldn't decide which wallpaper to choose for her room, whether to drop chemistry, or whether to join Spanish Club this fall.

"Bren! Jamie! Wait up!" a voice called behind them.

Morgan Cross, Maya's younger sister, ran up the midway, braids flying. She slid to a stop and grinned, showing off two brightly painted daisies, one on each brown cheek.

Jamie touched the cracked design with her forefinger. "Cute. Who's doing face painting?" she asked.

"The cheerleaders," Morgan replied. "Why aren't you there, Bren? The girl running it asked me if you were going to work."

Bren shrugged. She'd meant to sign up. She just hadn't been able to make a decision between an afternoon or an evening shift. "Where's the face-painting booth?" She looked around vaguely.

Morgan pointed to the end of the row they'd missed. "Down there. She'll be glad to put you to work. I don't think she's had lunch yet."

Bren grabbed Jamie's arm and pulled her toward the cheerleaders' booth. "Come with me," she urged. "It might be fun. Sure beats succotash."

Morgan's eyes bugged. "Yuck! Did you guys really eat succotash? What did you do that for? As soon as I find Alex, we're going to get elephant ears. Fair food's the best!"

Bren giggled and pointed her thumb at Jamie. "Jamie's the *Queen* of Succotash. She loves the stuff."

"I do not!" Jamie protested. "I just said that the fair was about . . ."

But Bren had already lost interest in succotash. "We gotta go, Morgan," she cut in. "See you later. Tell Maya I said hi!" She dashed toward the cheerleading booth, dragging Jamie with her.

"Hi Suzanne!" she greeted the girl with dark pixie hair running the booth. "I'm sooooooo sorry! I *really* meant to sign up! But there were so many times to pick from, and I didn't have the foggiest idea what was going to be happening this week and . . ."

Suzanne held up her hand to stop the tidal wave of apologies. "Take my place. Let me grab a veggie burger, and we'll call it even." She stood up, stretched, and pulled out a folding metal chair for Bren to take a seat.

"I'm going to go check out the horses, Bren," Jamie announced. "You work, and I'll be back later."

Bren plopped down in the chair and gave Jamie a pleading look. "But you're the artist! You'd be way better at face painting than I would." She stood back up. "Maybe I should do this tonight."

Jamie gave her a playful push. "Down girl! Down! I'm only going over to the barns—not to the mall. You know you'd hate it."

Bren sat. It was true—the smell of barns made her gag. But maybe there would be a cute guy there. On the other hand she might meet somebody even better if she stayed put. She sighed and looked at the list of designs she was expected to paint. *It's a good thing I'm the painter and not the paintee*, she thought. *If I had to pick one of these, my face would be so wrinkled by the time I made up my mind I'd be down to two choices—a spider or a road map.*

"Hey, you doing business, or not?" a cranky voice interrupted.

Bren looked up into the green shadowed eyes of a girl with hair the color of broccoli.

"I want a ladybug next to my eye and a long tulip that starts right underneath it and goes all the way down to my chin. Okay?" the green-haired girl asked.

"Sure." Bren motioned for her to sit in the empty customer's chair and picked up a small paintbrush. She dipped it in the red paint and made a small, tentative circle at her customer's temple. "You having a good time?" she asked for something to say. It was too weird touching a stranger's face without making conversation.

"Yeah." The girl nodded just enough to make Bren have to enlarge the red circle. "There's a palm reader over in the pavilion. She told me I'm going to take a trip soon. She's right too. My mom's boyfriend's supposed to take us to Japan."

Bren stopped painting and stared at the girl. "Are you kidding? This woman actually tells you what's going to happen in the future?"

"Sure." The girl cracked her gum and nodded again. "You ought to try it. It only costs a dollar."

Bren didn't reply. A surge of excitement raced up her spine. This was what she'd been looking for all summer—somebody to tell her what to do and stop this agonizing indecision. As soon as Jamie came back from the barn and the cheerleader finished her veggie burger, she jumped to her feet.

"Sorry—but I need to leave. I'll come back tomorrow," she promised. Before anyone could argue, she bolted out of the booth and headed down the aisle to the midway, almost breathless with excitement.

"Hey!" Jamie cried, running after her. "Where are you going? For somebody who can't make a decision, you're sure charged all of a sudden."

"I'm having my palm read. Come on!" Bren grabbed Jamie's arm and tugged her toward the long, white pavilion where the palm reader had set up shop.

"Oh, Bren, come on. Get real!" Jamie begged. "This is so stupid. You don't want to do this."

"Yes, I do."

"No, you don't. It's crazy. What in the world has gotten into you lately? All summer you've been so indecisive—and now look at you!"

Bren slowed down. "That's just it. Don't you get it?" she asked. "I've finally decided to do something about my indecision."

"But—"

"But nothing." Bren picked up the pace again. "Ever since I—" She stopped in mid-sentence. "Just wait—this is going to be way cool. I'm going to figure out my entire life."

"Whoa! Slow down! You started to say something. Ever since what?" Jamie demanded, following Bren inside and down the main aisle of the long building.

"Nothing." Bren scanned the signs. "There she is! And look—there's no line."

Before Jamie could stop her, Bren charged over to the palm reader's table and slapped down a dollar bill. "I'd like you to read my palm, please," she said.

The palm reader closed the paperback mystery novel she'd been reading and put the dollar in a battered tin box. "All right. Have a seat. I need your right hand." Her voice was flatter than an Indiana cornfield and not nearly as welcoming. Melted makeup pooled in the deep crevices by her mouth, and her hair looked big and sticky enough to trap the gazillion flies that buzzed around the inside of the building.

Bren slid into a folding chair and eagerly held out her hand. The palm reader took her slim, olive hand in her own fleshy one and traced a curvy line all the way down to the wrist.

"You have a long life line. You will live to see many grand-children," she said.

Bren glanced at Jamie and giggled. Jamie rolled her eyes.

"You are a girl for whom money is no obstacle," the palm reader continued. "It flows into your life as easily as the river flows to the sea."

Bren gasped and widened her eyes. That was so true! Her father ran a lucrative medical practice and indulged his only child's every whim.

"I see that you enjoy some type of outdoor sport."

Bren frowned. Except for tagging along on the swim team, just to hang with her friends, she didn't do sports. And anyway swimming was indoors. Her heart sank to the soles of her Steve Madden sandals.

"Ah, wait! Now I see what it is! Cheerleading. You are a cheerleader!" The palm reader exclaimed. "You will soon have wonderful success in this field."

Bren gasped again. Goosebumps played tag, up and down her arms. This woman had no idea what she'd just said. Or maybe she did—in which case she was so good it was scary. Bren shot Jamie a what-do-you-think-of-that look, but Jamie only frowned and shook her head.

The woman hunched over Bren's palm one last time, using the pointed end of a sharp red fingernail to follow a short line that intersected another short line to make a lopsided X. "It also appears that you will meet a tall, dark, handsome stranger," she offered. "You will know him by his blue intensity."

Bren blinked. "Blue intensity? Wh—what does that mean?"

The palm reader flashed a mysterious smile, dropped Bren's hand, and picked up her paperback. "When it happens, you will know. Until then you must trust."

Bren opened her mouth to ask what she was supposed to trust but then shut it again. Clearly, the only thing the palm reader wanted to read at this point was *The Mysterious Waters of Heebie-Jeebie Lake*—preferably without an audience. Bren stood up, confusion swirling around her like confetti in a windstorm. The cheerleading part of the fortune was so crystal clear she could practically see her reflection in it. But the blue intensity stuff was a mystery.

"See how stupid that was?" Jamie demanded as they headed back outside.

"But she knew about my father's money and that I was a cheerleader," Bren objected.

"Well *duh*," Jamie said, not bothering to hide her exasperation. "You're wearing Gap, and those sandals practically scream Saks. As for cheerleading, take a look at your collar."

Bren grabbed the pointed collar of her sleeveless pink top and stared at the tiny silver megaphone pinned to it. "This thing? Oh, it's so little she probably didn't even see it. What about my life line, huh?" She ran her finger along the same curvy line the palm reader had traced. "See? It's right here! No way did she make that up."

"Bren! Watch where you're . . . !"

Bren crashed headlong into something hard and muscular. She shrieked, jumped back—and locked gazes with eyes as blue as a brand-new pair of stonewashed jeans. Stunned, she spun on her heel and pointed wildly at her own eyes to get Jamie to notice them. Her finger jabbed her eyeball.

"Owwwwwwwwwwwwww!" she wailed. "I just poked myself in the eye!"

"Oh wow!" said the dark-haired stranger behind her. "That's intense."

chapter.2

Y ou're a walking disaster area," Jamie exclaimed, handing Bren a tissue.

"You okay?" the stranger asked.

Bren dabbed at her eye and nodded. "I'll live. I'm Bren Mickler, and this is my friend, Jamie Chandler."

The stranger grinned. "Glad to know you. I'm Tad Campbell. I play football for Lakeland."

Bren giggled, took one last swipe at her eye, and shoved the tissue in the pocket of her white shorts. "Then we probably shouldn't be seen talking to you," she teased. "I'm a cheerleader for Edgewood. We're playing you next Friday night."

"Yep," he agreed. "Too bad you're going to lose your first game of the season. You have my condolences." His eyes scanned Bren as he retrieved some papers that had fallen to the ground in the collision.

"What makes you so sure we're going to lose?" she demanded, crouching down to help.

"Because we have a better defense than you do." He flashed a slow, easy smile to soften the words. "Besides, Friday's the twenty-ninth, and twenty-nine just happens to be my lucky number."

Bren felt a prickle of interest. "Really? You believe in lucky numbers?" She stood up and glanced at Jamie who rolled her eyes again.

"Thanks," Tad said, taking the papers. "Sure. Doesn't everybody?"

"I don't," Jamie replied. She sounded snappish. Bren sent her a "be nice" look, but Jamie ignored it and set her mouth in a tight, disapproving line that made her look like a librarian in one of those old-timey black-and-white movies on AMC.

"Well, *I* believe in them," Bren offered. "At least I think I do." She pointed at the stack of papers in Tad's hand. "What are those?"

He ran a hand over his buzzed hair and snorted. "Just some descriptions of the antiques my mom dropped off at the fair. She's exhibiting like our whole house this year. It's really stupid. Would you believe you can actually win a ribbon for having the best, or the oldest, chair? Hey, you two want to come with me while I drop these off? Then we could grab something to eat. I'm starved."

Jamie shook her head. "Thanks, but I need to go find Maya. Bren, meet me at the entrance in an hour. I'm going to see if Maya will take us home."

"I'll take you home," Tad offered.

Jamie shook her head. "Thanks, but Maya will do it. We're both working tonight at the Gnosh." She referred to the fifties-style diner owned by Maya's father. To the high school crowd it was practically Command Central.

"Okay," Bren agreed. "I'll be there." She felt nervous being left alone with Tad, but she also wanted Jamie gone. First she'd disapproved of the palm reader, and now she was acting like it was some kind of crime to have a lucky number.

At the antiques booth, Tad handed his mother's descriptions to an elderly man and said that Helene Campbell had sent them. The man took the neatly printed pages, filled out a form, and handed it to Tad. "Here's your receipt, young feller," he said. "Don't lose it."

Tad folded the paper and stuffed it in his shirt pocket. "Come on," he said to Bren, "let's get some fries."

Bren followed him to the French fry stand, her mind whirring like an overworked computer. All summer she'd been struggling so hard with indecision, and nobody understood. Her friends thought it was just one more goofy Bren thing to add to a list that already rivaled the length of a foot-long sub. Even her parents didn't understand.

"Snap out of it Bren!" her mother said, only half teasing.

"This is ridiculous!" her usually understanding father agreed.

What they all didn't get was that ever since That Thing had happened in June it was like she was frozen. No matter how hard she tried, she couldn't make a decision about anything. But now in just one incredible afternoon, the perfect answer to the problem had crashed right into her. Or, she had crashed right into it. Or, rather, *him.*

"Want salt?" Tad asked handing her a greasy cup of crinkled fries.

Bren shook her head no and stepped out of the way to let him help himself from a plastic dishpan filled with salt and ketchup packets. How did a person figure out her lucky number she wondered. Did you somehow just know, or did you have to wait and see if something told it to you? Maybe it was a matter of reading the right book.

A sudden shower of something gritty on her bare toes cut her off in mid-thought. She stared down at her feet in disbelief. A small mound of salt straddled her big toe and the one next to it. Together they looked like two overseasoned appetizer wieners.

"What did you do *that* for?" she squealed, shaking her foot to knock off the salt.

"Sorry! I didn't mean to toss the whole packet." He looked

embarrassed. "I was just throwing salt over my shoulder for good luck."

Bren stared at him. Forget what she'd said about him being the answer to her problem. The guy was a certifiable nutcase!

"I'm sorry," he repeated. "I just got a little carried away. Come on. Let's eat, and then I'll make it up to you with a ride on the Ferris wheel." A slow, easy smile spread across his face like warm honey on a hot biscuit.

Bren's heart did a somersault. So he'd salted her toes a little. It wasn't the end of the world. Maybe there was even some basis to this salt tossing thing. Until today, she'd never considered the possibility of psychic phenomena, and now she'd met someone who could not only teach her but was also gorgeous in the bargain. As soon as they finished their fries, she jumped up and pointed to the Ferris wheel.

"Come on. You promised," she reminded him.

"Okay! Okay! But *you* have to promise not to rock the cart."

"*Me* rock the cart?" Bren demanded. "That's what guys do. Girls don't do that. Except maybe when they're with guys who don't want them to!" She tilted her head slightly to the right and gave him a 100-watt smile.

Tad took her empty French fry cup, crumpled it with one hand and tossed both his cup and hers into an open recycling bin. "You ever been on a double wheel?" he asked.

Bren nodded. "Once—in Ohio. Uh-oh!" She spun around

on one heel and speed-walked toward the Ferris wheel, forcing him to hurry to catch up.

"Hey, the thing's not gonna roll away!" he hollered, striding after her.

"I'm just anxious to get in line," she muttered, looking over her shoulder at the midway games. "I only have half an hour before I have to meet Jamie." Actually, she hadn't even thought of Jamie until that second. What propelled her down the midway was something far more compelling than Jamie Chandler.

Out of the corner of her eye, she'd spotted Jason Hersh and his friends tossing beanbags at milk bottles. When they'd last do-si-doed, he'd mentioned the possibility of them going to the fair together Saturday night for the tractor pull. At least that decision had been a no-brainer, Bren thought. But all she needed was to run into him—at the fair in the company of another guy.

Jason and his friends had given up on the milk bottles and were headed toward the rides. "You know what? I don't feel like riding the Ferris wheel after all," she said. "Let's stop by the cheerleading booth, and I'll introduce you to all the people who won't be rooting for you Friday night."

Tad laughed. "Okay," he agreed. "Lead on."

Bren ducked down the goat's milk fudge aisle and up the one next to it to the cheerleaders' table. Suzanne was painting a rainbow on Maya's cheek while Jamie advised about the proper color sequence.

"Hi!" Bren greeted her friends. "I want you guys to meet Tad Campbell. He plays football for Lakeland. Tad, this is Suzanne Kennedy doing the painting, and Maya Cross being painted. And of course you've already met Jamie."

"Hi, Tad," Suzanne murmured. She gripped Maya's chin, concentrating on the yellow arch she was painting on her cheek. Maya waved a hand sporting perfect bronze nails and rolled her eyes to indicate that she couldn't talk and be rainbowed at the same time. Jamie just nodded.

Suzanne filled in a bare spot on the yellow arch, then let go of Maya's chin and dipped the brush in a cup of water. "Hey Bren, I forgot to ask you before. Any chance you could let us use your laptop?" she asked. "It would be so much easier keeping track of stuff at the booth."

Bren shrugged. "Sure. I mean, maybe. I mean, of course you can. Unless—" She frowned. Ever since she'd met Tad Campbell, she'd been fine, and now one simple question had reduced her to a stuttering mass of uncertainty again.

"I think you can take that as a yes," Jamie said to Suzanne.

Bren tossed her a grateful look.

"Hey, Tad," Suzanne said as she wiped her paintbrush on an old towel. "Why don't you bring your friends over to the booth, and we'll paint your faces. We can do footballs, school colors.

Whatever you want. And it's for a good cause too. We need new uniforms."

Tad smiled the same slow, lazy grin that had made Bren's heart flip back at the French fry stand. "I might just do that," he said. "But right now I gotta make tracks. I'm supposed to be at football practice. If I don't get to the field on time, Coach will knock me off the starter list. Bren, I'll see you soon, okay?"

A delicious warmth surged up Bren's neck and spread over her face like sunlight. "Sure," she said, conscious of Suzanne's envious gaze.

As soon as Tad was out of earshot, both Suzanne and Maya pounced on her for details.

"He's so cuuuuuuuuuuuuute!" Suzanne moaned. "Bren, you have all the luck."

"What a hottie," Maya agreed. "Give us the scoop. Come on—tell all!"

Bren didn't reply. There was that word again—luck. Was there really such a thing as luck? And if there was, did she have it? And if she *did* have it, why had simple things like restaurant menus and movie listings become as intimidating as an exam in advanced calculus? But more important, why, if she was so lucky, had That Thing happened back in June? Lucky people didn't miss the opportunity of a lifetime.

"I guess it was just meant to be," she replied.

Jamie groaned. "See?" she demanded, turning to Maya.

"What did I tell you? She's losing it. Tell her that just because she crashed into a good-looking guy doesn't mean it was written in the lines of her palm."

Maya raised an elegant eyebrow. "I have to side with Jamie on that one, Madame Klutz. Your reputation precedes you."

"Oh yeah?" Bren countered. "Then tell me why he's tall, handsome, a stranger, and has blue eyes."

"Because he happened to be in the way?" Maya asked, putting her sunglasses on.

"Oh puh-leeeeeze!" Bren groaned. "The palm teller said I'd know him by his blue intensity. Did you *see* those eyes? And he even used that word—intense."

Maya barely managed to swallow a laugh. "Uh, Bren. Did you ever notice how many people in this world have blue eyes? As for intense, *all* the guys say that. Everything's intense to them. It's just an expression. Don't tell me you *believe* this weird junk? I thought you were more sophisticated than that."

"I am!" Bren protested. "I'm just saying that—"

Maya cut her off. "Hey, we gotta go girls! Jamie and I are gonna be late for work."

"Don't forget the laptop, Bren!" Suzanne called after them as they made their way down the aisle to the midway.

In the parking lot, Jamie and Maya complained good naturedly about all the ice cream they were going to have to scoop at the Gnosh, thanks to the blistering heat. Bren followed them across the gravel in a sulk. They acted so superior, like they knew everything there was to know about everything. Well, maybe there were a few things they *didn't* know.

A bright blue minivan pulled out of a parking space and sped past them toward the exit. Bren caught a quick glimpse of the driver and let out a triumphant yelp.

"*More* blue intensity!" she shouted. "That was Tad!"

"More coincidence," Jamie muttered.

"More nuttiness, if you ask me." Maya said firmly. She wagged a long, tapered finger in Bren's face. "Girl, if you don't get your head straight, you'll wind up *singin'* the blues!"

chapter.3

Late the following morning, Bren stared at her computer, watching the silver and magenta home page load. Maya's best friend, Amber, began TodaysGirls.com so the girls would have a private place to chat. Amber also posted her Thought for the Day there:

Your word is like a lamp for my feet and a light for my way. (Psalm 119:105)

God shines a flashlight on our path because we'd freak out if he beamed a laser and exposed our entire lives. Take each day as it comes and trust it will unfold according to His plan.

Bren sighed and read it again. Either this was the most amazing coincidence in the solar system or else Jamie had been blabbing about the fair. She clicked over to the chat room. The others—Amber, Jamie, Morgan, Alex, and Maya—were already there.

> **chicChick:** My ears R ringing. U talking about me?
>
> **faithful1:** Is the BLUEbird of happiness still perched on ur shoulder?
>
> **chicChick:** I knew it, Rembrandt! U talk 2 much!
>
> **rembrandt:** I'm only trying 2 make U get real!!!!!
>
> **jellybean:** I want 2 hear about the palm reader
>
> **chicChick:** No way! U guys don't d-serve any more info.
>
> **TX2step:** I hear the Psychic Friends Network is hiring. Need a job?
>
> **chicChick:** Ack! U R all making me crazy! The big issue is I 4got to give Tad my #.
>
> **nycbutterfly:** Not 2 worry. The stars say U'll run in2 him again. Literally!
>
> **chicChick:** Ha-ha. I'm going 2 work on my fashion page now. BBL--IF u get lucky.

Bren logged out of the chat and clicked onto her Smashin' Fashion page. She wanted to add something about the white leather skirt by Esprit she'd seen at the mall. Paired with a dark denim jacket, it totally rocked. Yet as hard as she tried, she couldn't concentrate on clothes not knowing when, or if, she'd see Tad again. When the phone rang ten minutes later, she lunged for it.

"Hey, Bren."

It was Jason Hersh. Her heart dropped back into her chest. She'd forgotten to call him back and still didn't know what to do about his hints for a date.

"Hi Jason. Listen, I was going to call you yesterday, but . . ."

"No problem. I was going over to the fair today, and Suzanne mentioned yesterday that you needed to bring your laptop over, so I thought maybe you could use a lift."

Bren's pulse quickened. She was dying to get over to the fair. And she *had* promised to bring the laptop. But it felt crummy to use Jason to get a chance to see Tad. But if she didn't see Tad . . .

"Hey, you there? How about if I pick you up at twelve-thirty?" Jason asked, slicing through the indecision.

"Thanks, that would be great," Bren replied. "See you then." Relief washed over her as she hung up the phone. Jason *wanted* to take her—she hadn't asked him. Which meant that she could now look for Tad with a conscience as clear as her face since she'd started using tea tree oil soap.

At the fair, Jason insisted on walking with her to the cheer-leading booth. She hoped he didn't plan to hang with her the whole day, but she couldn't very well be rude after he'd given her a ride in his silver Cabrio.

"I might have to work for a while this afternoon," she warned him as they turned down the aisle to the face-painting booth.

"That's cool," he replied. "We can hang out till then."

"Okay, sounds like fun," she agreed. He wasn't such a bad guy. He had a cute smile, and the little gap between his teeth made him look sort of sweet. It might even be fun to ride a few rides, maybe grab an ice cream cone—as long as there was still time to be with Tad.

"Hey, you brought your laptop!" Suzanne exclaimed as Bren and Jason came up to the booth. "That's great. Too bad we don't have any customers." She made a face. "Yesterday we did fine. But I found out it was because it was Kid's Day. Anybody under twelve got in free. Today there aren't as many rug rats, and the ones who are here would rather ride the rides. We'll be lucky to get new shoelaces, much less whole uniforms, at this rate."

Bren handed over her computer. "Bummer. Listen, do you mind if Jason and I walk around for a while? I can come back and work in an hour."

"That would be great." Suzanne opened the laptop and switched it on. "I need to get home early. Date tonight."

"So—what do you want to do?" Jason asked Bren as they walked out onto the midway.

Bren looked at the Ferris wheel, the carousel, and the bumper cars, and drew a blank. "Uh—I don't care. You decide."

He grinned. "I was hoping you'd say that! Come on—let's go up to the barns and check out the animals."

Bren scanned her light blue tank top, khaki shorts, and brand new wheat-colored sneakers. She'd taken such pains to look like she'd casually hopped out of the slick pages of *Teen* magazine. But she hadn't even been at the fairgrounds a half hour, and he wanted to turn her into a poster girl for *Farm Journal.* By the time she met up with Tad, her Tommy Girl would smell more like Tommy *Goat.*

"Great," she muttered. "What did you want to see especially?"

Jason beamed his cute gap-toothed grin. "The pigs!"

"The pigs," Bren repeated faintly. "That would definitely be *my* first choice."

He punched her lightly in the arm and laughed. "Come on—be a sport. You'll love the babies. Promise."

She seriously doubted it but allowed herself to be led into the reeking barn. When her eyes adjusted to the dim light, she let out a squeal and jumped back. "What *is* that thing—a rhinoceros?" she sputtered, pointing at an enormous hog. "It's almost as big as Maya's Volkswagen!" Okay, so it was an exaggeration. The hog was not the size of a small car, but it was still huge, filthy, and covered with stiff black hairs.

Jason laughed and reached across the wooden gate to scratch the grunting animal's ears. "This one's a porker all right," he agreed. "But come down here where they keep the Vietnamese pot bellies. You'll love 'em. They're all wrinkly, and their tails are straight as a board."

Bren stepped carefully down the straw-covered aisle to a pen where a medium-sized black pig lay surrounded by six round, squealing babies. A girl of about twelve sporting twin pigtails herself, flashed a silver smile at Jason. "Hey, Jay," she greeted him. "Would your friend like to hold one of the piggies?" She scooped up a squirmy little pig and held it out to Bren.

"Oh, no! I . . ." Bren protested.

The girl dumped the pig into Bren's arms. She held it out in front of her the way men hold babies in the movies. "I can't. I don't—" Her eyes gyrated wildly, begging Jason for help.

"It's all right. Here—hold it against you," he instructed, guiding the pig toward her. "It's just like any baby animal. When she grows up, she'll be 90 to 150 pounds, but that won't be for a while yet. Right now she's just a cute little yuppie puppy."

"A what?" Bren laughed nervously and looked down at the solid little body nestled against her.

Jason laughed. "Back in the eighties, pot-bellied pigs were a fad. The media started calling 'em yuppie puppies. This one belongs to my sister, Julie. Oh, by the way, Julie, this is Bren. Bren, Julie," he said, introducing her to the girl with the pigtails.

"Hi Bren," Julie said with another flash of braces. "You want to help clean her ears?"

"No, that's okay." Bren started to hand the pig back, then she reconsidered. Maybe she could just hold it a minute longer. The piglet was adorable—so sweet and trusting with its little feet waving in the air. But then again, even Tommy *Goat* would smell better than Eau de Swine.

On the other hand, holding the pig did feel a little like holding a baby—and it didn't smell as bad as some babies' diapers. But it was also getting late. If she didn't find Tad soon, she'd be stuck at the booth with no chance of seeing him unless he stopped by to have his face painted.

Julie poured a small dollop of olive oil into a plastic bowl, dipped a clean Q-tip into it, and offered the swab to Bren. "Here—sit down on this bale of hay and put her in your lap," she instructed. "Her name's Peggy Sue, by the way." She giggled at that. "You know—like the old Buddy Holly song. My dad's always singing it."

Bren rearranged Peggy Sue on her lap and took a quick look around the barn in search of Tad. Satisfied that he wasn't there, she took the swab, cupped a delicate ear in her hand, and gently rubbed the oil over the inside. Peggy Sue closed her eyes and grunted blissfully.

"See? She loves it!" Julie cried.

"Yeah," Bren agreed. She looked up at Jason and grinned. "Is this what you call pig heaven?"

"You bet!" he agreed, grinning back.

If pleasure could be measured in BTUs, he'd be radiating like a red-hot woodstove, Bren thought, suppressing a twinge of guilt. Clearly, he was a zillion times more interested in her than she was in him. She finished the pig's ears and handed Peggy Sue over to Julie.

"We really do have to go." She stood up and brushed the

straw off her clothes. "I want to try and find Jamie. She went over to where the art exhibits are. Do you guys know where that is?"

"Follow me," Jason said. "See ya Jules." He led the way out of the barns and over to another white building just like the one that housed the palm reader.

Bren trailed behind, her eyes scanning the crowd for Tad. He had to be here somewhere. He'd promised to see her tomorrow, and tomorrow was *now.*

Inside the arts building, Jamie spotted Bren and raced over, her ponytail swinging behind her like a clock pendulum. She grabbed Bren's arm and squeezed so hard her short nails left white half-moon indentations. "I'm going crazy!" she moaned "Guess who's here?"

Bren lit up. "Tad?"

Jamie let go of her arm. "Tad who? Oh, *him.* No, of course not. I'm talking about Garrett Lindstrom!"

"What's a Garrett Lindstrom?" Bren's gaze swept across the crowded room.

"Only about the most amazing painter on the planet!" Jamie gushed. "And guess what? He's here from New York for the next couple weeks and is having a seminar for aspiring artists. Maya took Alex and Morgan to get lunch, and then she promised to drive me home to get my portfolio. Pray he lets me in!"

"Why wouldn't he let you in?" Jason asked. "That street scene you had in the art show at school last year was cool. I really dug that rainy, moody look. You made Edgewood look like Paris."

"Thanks." Jamie's cheeks turned pink with pleasure. She looked over her shoulder at a tall, hawk-nosed man who stood frowning at a drawing handed to him by an anxious-looking girl. She kept yanking on the tail of her T-shirt like she was trying to keep from flying into orbit. "That's him," Jamie whispered, nodding in the direction of the man. "He's pretty scary. Doesn't seem to like anything. But I have to get in—I have to!"

"Don't worry. You're in!" Bren encouraged her. "Listen, if you need me, I'm over at the face-painting both." She glanced at her watch and yelped. "Ouch! I'm five minutes late already! Thanks for the ride, Jason. I'll catch up with you later."

Before he could protest, Bren dashed out of the arts building toward the booth. She thought about making a quick stop at the palm reader's building but decided against it. Maybe later she could slip away and have her fortune told again, but for now, she'd better show up ready to paint ladybugs and smiley faces.

"Business is still lousy," Suzanne announced when she got to the booth. "We had two cat faces, one smiley face, and an apple since you left. I got a newspaper if you want something to do." She handed over a copy of the *Edgewood Leader* and stood up. "I'm outta here—going miniature golfing tonight with some of the squad girls."

Bren gave her a sympathetic look. She's rather pet a hog than roll golf balls around. The last time she'd gone miniature golfing, she'd been so slow at the windmill that a line had formed all the way back to the ticket stand. She could still hear the bald man in the Hawaiian shirt hollering, "Hey girlie, either hit it or forget it!"

"Have fun," she said with a shudder.

"I will." Suzanne grabbed a tote bag and waved. "If you think of any other ways to make some cash, let me know."

As soon as she was gone, Bren munched on the squished Milky Way she'd stashed in her pocket and thumbed through the paper, one eye on the headlines, the other keeping a close watch on passersby. It wasn't until she came to the last page of section B that the *Edgewood Ledger* captured her full attention: *It's All in the Stars by Debbie Day.*

A horoscope column on the same page as the comics! The fine hairs on Bren's arms quivered. When she was little, she and her dad used to read Garfield and Peanuts, but these days she rarely glanced at the newspaper. Quickly, she folded it, laid it flat on the table, and used her forefinger to scan the listings. She was so jazzed, she had to read the prediction twice before it sank in.

Your progress cannot be stopped. That which was lost is found.

"Oh wow," she whispered aloud. Did it mean what she thought it meant? Of course. Tad wasn't exactly *lost*—she just didn't happen to know where he was at the moment. It was possible that Debbie Day was referring to the amethyst ring that had disappeared off Bren's dresser last week. She read the words a third time, searching every nuance for something—anything —that applied to Tad.

"Hey stargazer!" a male voice said right in front of her.

Bren startled, looked up—and felt herself drowning in a sea of blue.

"Sorry! Didn't mean to scare you. Want to read me my horoscope?" Tad Campbell asked. He had that just-showered look that made even huge teddy bear guys seem like little boys.

Bren breathed the fresh, woodsy fragrance of his cologne and felt almost dizzy. *If only Jamie and Maya could see me at this moment,* she thought, *I'd not only hold a pig—I'd kiss one!*

chapter.4

So—how's the face painting business?" Tad asked, looking around the empty booth.

"Not so good," Bren admitted. "Which is why I was reading the astrology column. Boredom."

"Astrology. Oh, I'm totally into that stuff." He picked up the newspaper and glanced at the horoscope column. "So what did it tell you about it?"

"Tell me about what?" For a second she was confused, then she realized he'd thought she'd been looking for information on the future of face painting. "Oh! You mean the business. I don't know. It doesn't exactly have a birth date, so it was a little hard to look up." She started to dismiss it, then thought of something that nearly propelled her out of her chair. "Wait a minute! Maybe it does. It was born two days ago. That would make it a Virgo."

She grabbed the newspaper back and scanned the column until she found Virgo. "'This could be your power play week,'" she read aloud. "'Focus on public relations, and your progress cannot be stopped.' That is so cool! Did you hear that?"

"What do you suppose it means?" Tad asked.

"I think it means we need to give the public what it wants," Bren replied. "Unfortunately, that doesn't seem to be face painting." She slumped in her seat and stared at the black lines of type. If only the predictions were a little clearer, it would be so much easier to know what to do.

Tad reached over and tapped the horoscope column. "Why not give people the future?"

"You mean like predictions?" Bren felt herself perking back up. "But there's already a palm reader over there." She waved in the direction of the white building. "And anyway, I don't know how to predict anything."

Tad grinned and tapped the laptop on the table. "If you could get the fair people to move you to where there's phone access you could hook up to the Internet and pull the predictions off there. I know some awesome sites. That palm reader would be yesterday's news. Tell you what." He reached into his pocket and pulled out a dollar bill. "I'll get you started. You read me my fortune from that newspaper, and I'll be your first customer."

Bren giggled. "Okay. What's your sign?" It sounded so eighties, she giggled again.

"Capricorn." He handed her the dollar bill, crossed his arms, and waited.

Bren cleared her throat. "'Enjoy yourself, and you will win big,'" she read. She looked up at him and raised her eyebrows, waiting for a reaction.

"Okay, *fair* enough. Ha-ha! *Fair!* Get it? That was an unintentional pun." He grinned in that dopey way jocks grinned when they were answering questions on TV. She could just see him ten years from now on ESPN playing in the NFL.

Bren groaned. "I got it. But I know you don't think this has anything to do with the fair. You think it's about the game next Friday."

Just as she was about to needle him about the dangers of overconfidence, Jamie whirled into the booth with Maya and Amber in tow. Jamie looked like a trick snake ready to explode from a can.

"Oh, Bren it was so awful!" she wailed, flopping down into the empty customer's chair. "Garrett Lindstrom is the rudest man in the world. He hates me. Or at least he hates my work."

"That's not true," Maya protested. "I was right there, and all he said was that you need to expand your horizons and work in more media. He's partial to pastels, and you didn't have any. It's not a big deal. You're in."

Jamie rubbed both hands over her face and shook her head. "Yeah, I'm in. But he made it clear he doesn't think I'm worthy of it. I think he felt sorry for me. Maybe I shouldn't do the workshop. I'll just end up being humiliated. The rest of the people he chose are in college already." She stood up and yanked her baseball cap over her eyebrows. "I'm not doing it," she declared. "I just won't show up, and I'll steer clear of the art building for the rest of the week."

"You most certainly will *not*," Bren protested. "At least not until we look up your fortune in this astrology column." She held out the newspaper for Jamie to see.

Jamie threw her arms in the air. "Not *that* again!" she moaned. "I mean it Bren Rhiannon Mickler, this is getting old. First palm readers and now astrology! What will it be next—tea leaves?"

Bren jumped up from her chair and waved the newspaper in front of Jamie, momentarily forgetting about Tad. "For your information, predictions are what will save this rotten face-painting fiasco. As a matter of fact, I'm going over to the fair office right this minute to see about getting us moved, so we can have Internet access to psychic sites."

Maya, Jamie, and Amber all talked at once—three voices pelting protests like spitballs. Bren covered her ears and glared at them. "Do you realize that you're creating a scene?" she said flatly. "And you don't even know what you're talking about. Also, this is a cheerleading project, and none of you are cheerleaders. Which means you don't get a vote."

"I think we do know what we're talking about, Bren," Amber said evenly. She took the newspaper, glanced at the column, and tossed it down on the table.

Bren turned to Tad for help. Somewhere in the midst of all the arguing, he had disappeared. She turned back to her friends, a sick feeling already forming in the pit of her stomach. "Will you guys please stay here and watch the booth?" she pleaded. "I need to find Tad. I know you think this is dumb, but it's really not a big deal. Jamie, I'm sorry I went nuts. Just sit here, and I'll be right back, and we can talk about it, okay?"

Jamie sat back down. "Okay," she agreed. "But I'm still not taking the seminar."

"We'll talk about it in a second," Bren promised. "You guys just stay put."

Bren hurried up the row of booths toward the midway, looking right and left for Tad. She was afraid that he'd been so turned off by all the fighting and everybody making fun of astrology that he'd left the fairgrounds. She sighed, knowing she had no way to contact him. The fair office was just ahead. She figured she might as well duck in while she had the chance and see if the cheerleaders could change locations.

A blast of cold air from a noisy window air conditioner hit her full force the second she opened the door of the one-room building. Phones shrilled, a fax machine sputtered out a message, and a radio blared the Dixie Chicks. Four women sat working at scarred metal desks.

"Excuse me," Bren hollered. "But is there any chance that the Edgewood cheerleaders could move to a location with Internet access?"

The woman at the closest desk looked at her like she'd just suggested setting up a face-painting booth on Pluto. "You're kidding, right?" she asked, sucking furiously on a mint.

"No, I'm serious," Bren persisted. "We aren't making any money, and we need to move."

The woman tossed down the pen she'd been using to mark her progress through a long column of numbers and shoved her damp hair off her forehead. "Why does everybody think we can work miracles around here?" she demanded. "The week of the fair is not the time to be asking for changes."

Bren wavered. Before she could decide whether to keep insisting, a younger woman with hair that looked like it had been trimmed with hedge clippers came to the rescue. "It's okay Millie," she interrupted. "They can go in the Industry Expo building. That aluminum siding place pulled out, remember?"

Bren smiled gratefully. "We'll take it!" she said before Millie could object. "How soon can we move?"

The woman with the spiky hair shrugged. "You can move right now for all I care. The phone's already there. Take your computer over and hook her up." She swiveled around in an ancient brown office chair, pulled a site map of the building from a stack of handouts on the table behind her, drew a big red X on it, and handed it to Bren. "There you go. X marks the spot."

Bren thanked her and left before Millie could object.

Slowly, she walked back to the face-painting booth, wondering whether Tad had been scared off permanently. By the time she arrived, Morgan and her friend Jared had joined Maya, Jamie, and Amber. Bren sighed. She wished she could wave a magic wand and make them all disappear.

"Bren!" Morgan called. "Jamie says you guys have a new idea to make money for your uniforms."

Bren glared at Jamie. "Yeah. We're going to use the computer to read fortunes." She picked up her laptop, snapped the cover shut, and looked around for something to write on. She needed to make a sign to let any fairgoers who actually wanted their faces painted know where to get it done.

"You went to see about moving, didn't you?" Maya demanded, staring hard at Bren.

Bren ignored her. "You guys going to help, or what? We got space in the Industry Expo building. It's not the best, but since we don't have wireless technology, we have no choice."

"I'll help you move," Morgan offered.

"Me too," Jared agreed. He reached in his pocket and handed Bren four quarters. "Could you tell my fortune first though?"

Bren shook her head. "Not yet. I need to scope out the Internet sites first. All I could do now is read what it says in the newspaper."

"That's okay," Jared said. "Do that."

Bren gave her friends a smug look and asked Jared his birth

date. Then she looked up April fifth. "You're an Aires," she told him. "It says here, 'As always, trouble comes from Scorpio.' Who do you know that's a Scorpio? That's October twenty-third to November twenty-first."

Morgan's eyes bugged. "That's *me!*" she yelped. "I'm a Scorpio. And that's just plain not true. Is it Jared? We don't fight. We get along great. This is stupid. I hate it!"

Jared looked at Morgan and muttered, "Yeah, that's right, Me and Morgan are good friends. The *best,*" he added. "Keep the dollar Bren, but I don't think this works."

"Ha-ha! What did we tell you!" Jamie crowed. "Get out of that one, Oh Mighty Seer."

Bren grabbed a piece of cardboard and dipped a brush in red paint. With broad angry strokes she painted, "Moved to Industry Expo." When she was finished, she taped it to the front of the table and gathered up the painting supplies. "Just because Morgan and Jared are friends doesn't mean that they can't have problems," she snapped.

"Oh, now *there's* a reach!" Amber snorted.

"Yeah, it never said anything about them having problems. It said they weren't compatible *ever,*" Jamie agreed.

Bren ignored her. Her eyes were riveted on Tad, who was coming down the midway carrying an enormous pink bear the size of the hog in the pig barn. He walked up to the booth grinning like a gecko and thrust his prize into Bren's arms.

"For my lucky lady," he said, "who called it right on the

money. I went to the ring toss and got big-time lucky. Just wait till tomorrow—I'll be back with the guys from the team! Those uniforms are guaranteed. Edgewood might have a bad season, but at least you girls will be great-looking losers."

"Hah!" Bren shouted from behind the bear. "So what do you know-it-alls say to *that?*"

Maya shook the bear's front paw. "I say, glad to meet you big pink bear. Too bad you're going home with a crazy woman!"

chapter.5

Bren wrinkled her nose at the black leather purse. "Too geezer-y," she told Amber. "Get this plaid bag. It totally matches that skirt you just bought, and it looks just like a Dolce and Gabbana."

"It does?" Amber reached into her shopping bag, pulled the skirt partway out, and held it up to the slick fabric of the plaid shoulder bag. "Oh, you're right—it's perfect. But there's hardly anything else I could use it with."

Bren sighed. "Quit being so practical. It's on sale."

She, Amber, and Maya had descended on the mall at 10 A.M. sharp in a frenzy of back-to-school shopping. For once, Bren had been reluctant to go. Predictions were outselling face painting ten to one at the fair ever since Tad had hooked her up to a really cool astrology site.

At first, some of the cheerleaders had been annoyed about the move to the Industry Expo building, figuring kids would never go in there. But once word spread about the high tech advice, the girls on the squad had not only stopped complaining but had also put Bren in charge of the entire project.

"Okay, I'll buy it," Amber murmured. She picked up a pair of red plaid earrings and held them up to Bren. "Over the top?"

"*Tres chic!*" Bren assured her.

While Amber paid for her purchases, Bren and Maya moved out of the boutique and into the mall to wait. They sat on the edge of the fountain and watched as crowds of teenagers mobbed past in both directions.

"Ewwww!" squealed Bren. "This fountain smells like about a gazillion fish live in it." She waved her hand beneath her nose.

"There aren't any fish in that fountain," said Maya. "It's that leftover tuna sandwich you're dragging around that stinks. I told you not to save it."

Bren sniffed the bag with the sandwich. "I think you're right," she said. "I just thought I should keep it, in case I get hungry at the fair later."

"You sure you need to go back to the fair after this?" Maya asked. "I was kind of hoping we could catch a movie. Our days of freedom are about to end."

Usually that was Bren's back-to-school line, but with predictions raking in money like autumn leaves, she felt charged with energy and excitement. School seemed light-years away.

"Sounds tempting, but no can do," she answered. "In fact, I really need to hit the road." She glanced at her watch. "Well, maybe I could stay another hour, but that's it."

"Bren!"

Bren's heart skipped a beat as she looked toward the shops on the other side of the mall. Tad Campbell was fighting his way through the crowd in front of Old Navy.

Maya crossed her legs and heaved a sigh. "Oh goodie, Mr. Psychic himself," she muttered.

Bren ignored her. "Hi Tad!" she called. "What are *you* doing here?"

Tad made his way over to them and sat down next to Maya. "My mother insisted I get a couple of shirts." He held out an American Eagle bag and shrugged indifferently. "You girls got time for a coffee?"

"I don't drink coffee," Maya muttered. "Bad for the complexion."

"Me either," Bren said, "but I could use a peppermint tea." She gave Maya a pleading look.

"Peppermint tea *does* sound good," Maya murmured, sounding about as convinced as a snake riding a unicycle. "Great!" Tad stood up just as Amber came out of the boutique. "Let's go to Starbucks."

Bren introduced him to Amber, who looked even less enthusiastic than Maya about going for tea. But she followed along to the coffee shop and even snagged them an empty table.

"You know, I was thinking, Bren," Tad said as they arranged their shopping bags and sat down. "If you want to really make some money at the booth, you might try adding something extra. Something new. Like maybe a tarot card reader."

"Oh, yeah, that'd be great!" Bren agreed. She didn't know a tarot card from an Old Maid card, but her eyes pleaded with Maya not to say so.

"Tea. I need tea!" Maya moaned, grabbing her throat like a lost traveler marooned in the Sahara at high noon

Tad laughed and stood up. "Just something to think about," he said to Bren. "I'll go get the drinks. Three peppermint teas and a latte."

As soon as he was gone, Maya and Amber attacked like a pair of rabid dogs. "Do *not* even think about it," Amber hissed, leaning across the table. "I'm serious, Bren. This is not stuff you want to mess with. Remember my quote for the day?"

"Amber's right," Maya agreed. "Let that lamp light those pedicure-perfect tootsies of yours and forget this lunacy. I mean it girlfriend. I want you to promise us here and now you will not get involved with tarot cards."

Bren looked baffled. "Okay, I promise. There's no time anyway."

If only she could admit the stupid thing that had happened back in June, maybe they'd stop ragging on her, she thought. But it was so monumentally dumb she cringed every time she thought of it.

Everybody was always laughing about the crazy scrapes she got into, but this time it was more than a scrape. One bad choice had cost her something valuable. When Tad came back, she changed the subject to football, and the tension drifted off in the steam from his latte.

"If we're going to get you back to the fair, Bren, we need to get moving," Maya said after half an hour of friendly banter.

"I'll walk out with you," Tad offered. He stood up and helped Bren consolidate her shopping bags. "I'm parked in the east lot."

"So are we." Bren gave him a dazzling smile and positioned herself to walk beside him as the group headed for the exit.

Tad pushed the mall door open and stepped outside, holding it open for the girls. Bren walked out first, followed by Maya, and then Amber. Just as Amber came through, Tad let out a shout that launched Bren into the air like a missile.

"Bren! Watch it! There's a black cat!"

"What? Where? *Why?*" For a split second, she was confused. Then she remembered—it was bad luck to let a black cat cross your path. She ran back toward the open door just as the thin cat raced across the strip of grass in front of LensCrafters and zipped in front of her.

"Noooooooooooooo! Noooooooo! Get away! Shoo! Shoo!" she cried, fanning her hands in the air. A shopping bag whapped her in the nose.

Bren leaped to the left. The cat leaped left, too, then charged toward her feet. If it was bad luck to have a black cat cross your

46

path, having one wrapped around your ankles must mean a total meltdown, she thought.

She screamed and hop-stepped backward. The heel of her right clog slammed down hard and crushed the cat's tail. Howling sharply, the cat clamped its pointy little teeth around her anklebone. It was like being kissed by a piranha.

"No Bren! Look out!" Maya hollered.

Bren vaulted back and fell off the curb in a heap. For a second, she lay sprawled on the concrete surrounded by shopping bags. The cat hadn't bitten her too hard. It was more of a nip than an actual bite, but she felt assaulted, humilated—and doomed. As the tiny creature leaped over her, he planted a black paw squarely in the middle of her chest like Alexander the Great claiming Macedonia.

"Are you okay?" Tad called. He ran to help her up. Dozens of legs passed, going in and out of the mall. A few of their owners snickered.

Bren scrambled to her feet, grabbed her bags, and dropped them again. Her face burned. "I'm fine," she muttered. "Just get that beast out of here!"

"He's hardly a beast," said Amber. "He's just some poor stray that someone dumped in the parking lot. He's more worried about finding his next meal and not getting run over than he is about giving you so-called bad luck! Besides, you squashed *his* tail."

"Here kitty, kitty," Maya called. "Oh, poor thing. Look how thin he is."

The cat sauntered back toward Maya, who scratched his ears. Maya grabbed the bag with Bren's sandwich. "He just smelled that stinky sandwich of yours," Maya glared over the rim of her glasses at Bren. "Here you go kitty," she said, pinching the tuna into small bites. The starving cat choked it down, hurriedly.

Bren mumbled something about seeing Tad later and fled to the car.

"You can't blame the cat, Bren," Maya said when everyone had piled into Mr. Beep. "If you hadn't spazzed, none of that ever would have happened."

Bren, who had climbed into the backseat, didn't say a word. All the way to the fairgrounds, she listened while Maya rambled on about the absurdity of old wives' tales. She somehow segued into a diatribe about how astrology was dead wrong because it was completely based on the earth's being at the center of the planetary system.

"By the time Copernicus figured out that the sun was actually in the center, astrology had been around forever, and nobody wanted to change it," Maya explained, hanging a left into the fairgrounds. "It started in ancient Babylon and spread to Egypt and then later to Rome and Greece. But it's completely nonscientific. In a word—it's bogus, baby."

"You don't have to convince *me*," Amber agreed.

Bren crossed her arms and stared out the window. They were welcome to think anything they wanted to think. Other people didn't happen to agree—a fact she saw proven the minute she walked into the Industry Expo building. A line beginning at the cheerleaders' computer snaked all the way back to the exit.

"Bren! I thought you'd never get here!" Suzanne cried when she saw Bren. "I didn't know what to do."

Bren took her place behind the computer and typed in the Internet address of the psychic site. Once it loaded, she smiled at the first customer in line and asked for her birth date. For the next hour and a half, she worked like a robot, handing out fortunes like cheese samples at the grocery store.

"You will reach a decision regarding a partnership," she told a Taurus who played on Tad's team.

"Thanks!" the guy said. "Just what I wanted to hear."

The next person in line was also a Taurus. "You will reach a decision regarding a partnership," Bren repeated. The thought crossed her mind that it was strange how all these Tauruses had partnerships in need of decisions, but she dismissed it and kept working.

"Do mine now," Suzanne urged when there was a lull. Suzanne had been busy with the face-painting business, which had livened up when people realized it provided something to do while they waited for their fortunes. "I'm an Aquarius."

Bren already knew the day's fortunes by heart, but she pretended to look it up to make Suzanne feel like she was getting her dollar's worth. "No matter what you do, you will come out on top," she reported.

Suzanne's eyes widened. "Really? That's so cool! For real Bren—you have no idea!"

Bren smiled. She'd given out that fortune at least fifty times already. She wondered about the odds of all of them coming true, but the thought was cut short when Alex and Morgan wandered up to the table.

"Come get pizza with us, Bren," Morgan urged. "They have that Greek kind you like with spinach and olives."

Bren wavered. The musky-salty ripe taste of black Kalamata olives made her mouth water. "Better not," she said reluctantly. "It's been awfully busy. Which reminds me—how are you and Jared getting along?"

Morgan frowned. "Don't you start that astrology junk again," she warned. "We're fine and we're going to stay . . ."

"Hey Bren," Alex cut in, "did I tell you my mom might be coming for a visit?" A tangled web of family problems back home in Texas required Alex to live in Edgewood with her grandparents. If her mother were planning a trip east, Bren knew it qualified as a big event, because money was tighter for the Diaz family than the knot in a cattle rope.

"That's great, Alex," she said, genuinely happy for her friend. "Want me to see what the stars have to say about it?"

Alex snorted. "No thanks. She's coming by Greyhound, not spaceship."

Bren stuck out her tongue at Alex and looked over at the door. Jamie had just sailed through it and was bounding over to the table looking stressed. "Bren, I need you to come shopping with me," she said without even saying hi.

Bren's eyes popped. *Jamie,* shopping? She looked around the large room and saw a crowd of kids coming toward them. No way should she leave—but Jamie wanting to shop? That was something she couldn't pass by.

"Morgan, help me out here," she pleaded. "All you have to do is ask people their birth date, scan this list, and read what it says. It's easy."

"We won't be gone long," Jamie promised.

Morgan sat down in Bren's chair looking like she'd been asked to translate *War and Peace* from the original Russian. But she bravely asked the first person in line for his birth date and handled the transaction without a hitch.

"So how are we getting to the mall?" Bren asked after she was sure it was safe to leave Morgan in charge. "Maya?"

Jamie shook her head no. "We're not going to the mall. We're going to the flea market."

Bren looked back at the booth longingly. She should have known better than to think Jamie had been gripped by a Gap attack. "Where's the flea market?"

"In the field next to the fairgrounds. We have our hand stamps, so there's no problem going in and out."

"Was there—uh—something you were especially hoping to buy?" Bren asked, trying to sound enthusiastic.

Jamie nodded. "I need to get an Etch-A-Sketch. Garrett

Lindstrom was talking about the amazing art people are doing with them. It sounds a little weird, but then *he's* a little weird."

Bren started to suggest she buy a new one but caught herself. Jamie didn't have money to toss around for toys, even ones that would further her art career.

"Okay, then," she agreed, as they stepped into the noon glare, "the flea market it is." She was so relieved that Jamie had mustered her courage and joined the seminar that she'd shop at a Turkish bazaar if it would help.

She followed Jamie out of the fairgrounds and across a stubbly field of sharp overgrown grasses to an open-air marketplace. Pick-up trucks, pup tents, and long metal tables sagging under the weight of old clothes, battered furniture, and chipped china circled the perimeter like a wagon train. Bren fought the urge to scratch imaginary itches and watched in amazement as Jamie sorted through the "merchandise" with the enthusiasm of a shopping spree winner at Bloomingdale's.

"Don't you love old things?" Jamie asked, admiring an ancient beaded evening bag sporting a silvery chain handle and six inches of dirty silver-gray fringe. Missing beads left random holes in what had once been an elegant floral design. "Don't you wonder where they've been, or who once owned them?"

The thought had never crossed Bren's mind. Junk was junk—who cared who once owned it? But it felt so good seeing her friend unwind, she was happy to tag along. Jamie abandoned the pile of ratty purses and moved on to another table heaped with grimy toys. Bren jammed her hands in her pockets and tried not to think of the gazillion microscopic organisms crawling all over the stuff. She stood back and watched as Jamie moved piles of games and naked dolls to see what lay hidden underneath.

"Bren! Look! An Etch-A-Sketch!" she squealed. She held up the red plastic screen as though she'd hauled up the treasure of the Titanic. "And it even works. Will you take a dollar-fifty for this?" she asked the owner.

Bren grinned and looked idly at the remaining merchandise while Jamie and the dealer dickered. A clear glass globe caught her eye, glinting in the bright noon sun. Before she could consider the germ factor, her hands reached out with a will of their own and picked it up. Carefully, she rotated it, expecting flakes of fake snow to waft around the pink plastic fairy sitting on a brown plastic toadstool inside.

"Don't worry—the answer is yes," a sweet, high-pitched voice said. The dealer who was bagging Jamie's Etch-A-Sketch glanced over. "That's Fairy Fortune," she commented. "Very popular in the 60s. You ask her questions, and she tells the future."

Bren felt an adrenaline rush. For once there was no decision to be made. Germs or no germs—she had to have this thing!

"I'll take it!" she said firmly.

Beside her she, could feel Jamie bristle, but she ignored it. Fairy Fortune was the extra advantage Tad said they needed at the booth. And she'd been waiting in the most unlikely spot in the universe.

"Will you make us a ton of money?" she mentally asked the yellow-haired figure as she rotated the globe again.

"Don't worry. The answer is yes."

chapter.6

Bren yawned and stretched across the sectional sofa in her bedroom, her painted toes tickled the Elmo doll at the sofa's curve. The *Happy Days* marathon had been flashing across her big-screen TV since noon, and she was starting to get tired of Fonzie.

Do girls today still think he's hot? she wondered. *Girls today . . . TodaysGirls! I'm supposed to be online right now!* She jumped off the couch and logged onto the site.

> chicChick: sorry I'm late! what's up?
> nycbutterfly: the sun, the moon, the stars
> TX2step: Your hopes, goofy though they R
> chicChick: play nice!
> rembrandt: Get serious U guys! I don't know what 2 do

about Garrett Lindstrom. 2day he told me my paint-
ings lack depth

chicChick: I can help U! I found a site that will cast your
complete horoscope. I will buy a horoscope 4 U--4 all
of U.

nycbutterfly: hear that noise? it's us--GROANING
LOUDLY

Bren logged off, annoyed at her friends. She was trying to
show them that she cared about their lives—Jamie's workshop
woes, and Alex's impending visit from her mom—and all they
could do was make jokes. She clicked idly over to Amber's
Thought for the Day and moaned aloud.

**God is our God forever and ever. He will guide us from
now on. (Psalm 48:14)**

**If we trust that God is at the helm, steering us to port,
we don't have to worry about the future. Our boats will
stay afloat! Cool, huh?**

Bren stared at the words, knowing that, once again, they
were meant for her. It infuriated her, the way Amber felt
impelled to single her out. Like nobody else needed help! She
picked up her magic fairy ball and wandered downstairs, glad to
leave them behind for a while.

In the family room, she flopped down on the end of the sectional where her mother sat reading the latest Michael Crichton novel.

"Hi honey. What's that you have?" Mrs. Mickler asked, looking up from her book

Bren smiled and held out the glass globe. "Just a thing I bought with Jamie at the flea market today. Ask a yes or no question, and Fairy Fortune will give you an answer."

Mrs. Mickler laughed. "Is it going to rain? Because if it is I better go get the cushions off the patio furniture."

Bren shook her head. "No! Not that kind of question. Something you really want to know—like your future."

"Oh Bren! You don't really believe that a toy can accurately predict what's going to happen in your life! You're too smart for that," Mrs. Mickler replied.

Bren scooted closer to her mother. "Come on!" she urged. "Just for fun—try it, okay?"

"To tell you the truth, there's not much I want to know. But okay—how's this? Will Dad make it home on time tonight so we won't be late for dinner with the Wilsons?"

Bren groaned as she turned over the ball. "This is not possible," the sweet voice announced.

"I sure didn't need any Fairy Fortune to tell me *that!*" her mother laughed.

"So ask it something else then," Bren persisted.

"No thanks. I'd rather take things as they come. What is this—a new craze, or phase, or something?"

Bren shook her head. "Of course not! It's practically an antique. It's from the sixties. I just kind of liked it. It's not like a big deal."

"Well then, have fun with it, sweetie." Mrs. Mickler stood up, planted a kiss on top of her daughter's head, and headed out the French doors to the brick patio for the cushions.

Bren watched her through the glass and fought an urge to howl and fling objects. Everybody acted like fortune-telling was either ridiculous or a cute little phase she'd grow out of. Didn't it occur to anybody that maybe there was a *reason* why she couldn't make her own choices anymore? It was bad enough that her friends were unsupportive, but the words *phase* and *craze* made her crazy.

She flounced back to her room with Fairy Fortune. Flopping down on the chair in front of her computer desk, she held the glass globe up to the overcast sky framed by the window.

Maybe it *was* silly to think that a toy, or even the stars, could tell her what to do. Maybe it really wasn't trusting God. But the predictions had been right—at least a lot of them had. Bren sighed and thought back to the early part of the summer when she'd made the worst choice of her life.

Just before vacation, the buzz around school had been that Ms. Malarkey, the cheerleading advisor, would select a new captain at the cheerleading camp held each year at the local college.

"Word is, it's yours, Bren," two of the girls on the squad had whispered during study hall. "But you have to be at camp, or she'll change her mind. She's a total freak about camp."

Bren's stomach had twisted into a pretzel. She'd been planning to skip camp this year in favor of a fashion design course at
the art museum, led by two designers from DKNY. She'd sent in
her portfolio and had been granted a quick acceptance. Best of
all, someone had scrawled on top of the letter: "Nice work! You
show promise!"

Cheerleading or fashion design? For two agonizing weeks,
the choice had been uncertain. First one side would shoot up,
then the other, as she'd considered the pluses and minuses of
each decision. In the end, she'd chosen cheerleading. There
would be other workshops, she'd reasoned, but the chance to be
head cheerleader might never come again.

"Stupid, stupid, stupid!" Bren muttered now, slamming
Fairy Fortune down on the desk harder than she meant to. She
checked for damage and breathed a sigh of relief to find there
wasn't any. Holding the globe in her hands again, she focused
her gaze on the sweet face of the little fairy.

"Was it dumb to choose cheerleading camp over the fashion
design course?" she whispered. Slowly, she turned the globe over.

"I'm sleepy now. Please ask me later," the syrupy voice replied.

Bren stared. She'd never heard *that* before. Annoyed, she set
the toy back on her desk and crossed her arms. Of course it had
been stupid. After what had happened, only a total dimwit
would argue otherwise. The phone interrupted her angry
thoughts.

"Hello," she said flatly.

"Bren, hi. Jason here. Is something wrong?"

Bren sighed. "No, just tired."

"Oh, that's good. That you're okay I mean. Listen, I never got to ask you at the fair, but would you like to go to the dance after the game next Friday?"

Bren picked up Fairy Fortune. She could practically feel the warmth of Jason's smile emanating through the little holes in the receiver.

"Yeah, it's the first dance of the year, and I thought it might be fun . . ." His voice trailed off.

Bren ignored him as she phrased the question in her head for the ball. *Should I go to the dance with Jason?*

She started to turn the ball over when she noticed something on her computer screen. An e-mail with an unfamiliar address had popped up. She set the ball down, clicked opened the message, and swallowed a squeal of excitement.

Hey Bren! Got your e-mail address from Suzanne. You on here now? Wanna IM? Tad

"Bren?" Jason asked in her ear. "Did you hear what I said about the dance?"

Bren forced her mind back to the phone. "Yes, I heard," she replied. "I was just thinking about it. I don't know—sometimes the early dances aren't so great. Last year they had a really bad DJ the first week." She was stalling for time. Of course she wanted to go to the dance. It was a matter of who she went to the dance *with*.

She hit *Reply* and typed:

I'm here Tad! I'll add you to my IM list right now.

"I don't really care too much about the DJ," Jason said as her fingers flew over the keys. "You don't really care that much, do you? Hey—are you typing?"

Bren hit *Send*. "Just finishing up an important message," she murmured. She added Tad's name to her Instant Messenger list. As soon as it was entered she e-mailed him, and he responded immediately with an instant message.

"Bren, do you want me to call back later?" Jason asked when the silence grew to the size of Garrett Lindstrom's ego.

He sounded a touch cranky.

"Huh? Um, no, yes, um . . ." Bren stared at the screen, transfixed.

Hey, Stargazer! Tell me—will I get my heart's desire?

Bren could almost here him speaking the words again. *If it's a relationship with me, yessssssssssss!* she thought.

"Yes? You'll go?" Jason screamed in her ear. "That's great!"

She ignored him and asked Fairy Fortune whether Tad would get his heart's desire.

"Your wish will be granted," the sweet voice replied.

"Who's there?" Jason asked. "I hear talking. Where can I meet you after the game?"

"Nobody," Bren replied ignoring the last question. Once again, her fingers flew over the keys. She hoped Tad would be as thrilled as she was to learn that their future relationship was guaranteed. His reply popped up at once.

Cool. Way to go, baby!

She wanted to jump up and down.

"I *said,* where do you want to meet after the game?" Jason persisted.

For a second Bren was confused. Then it dawned on her. She had herself a date for the dance. With the wrong guy.

chapter.7

Bren surveyed herself critically in the full-length mirror. The outfit she'd selected lacked a certain indefinable something. She squinted then revolved slowly, pretending she was Tad, who would be on her doorstep in less than ten minutes. Last night he'd asked her to accompany him on some mysterious adventure. She turned back around to the front and stared at her reflection. Perfect hair. Perfect makeup. Perfect style. No color.

Quickly, she unbuttoned the white knit tee with the heart-shaped neckline. The white capris could stay, but an occasion charged with this much potential needed a jolt—and she had just the fire-engine-red three-quarter-sleeve top to provide it. She pulled open a drawer, rummaged through the neatly folded stacks of clothes, and yanked it out. Against her dark coloring the bright crimson popped.

"Bren! Your guest is here!" her mother called from downstairs.

Bren glanced at the clock. He was early—a good sign. She smoothed the top down over the white capris, admiring the way the clingy fabric showed off her narrow waist. There was only one problem. What would she do if—make that *when*—he asked her to the dance at his school after the game? She hadn't had the heart to tell Jason she'd never meant to agree to the Edgewood dance.

"I'll be right down!" she called. She picked up Fairy Fortune and considered how to phrase her question. It was such a pain the way the ball only gave yes or no answers.

"Will Tad ask me to the dance?" she whispered.

"Sorry, I'm not prepared to answer right now!" the voice replied.

Bren sighed and put the ball in her canvas tote bag to take to the fairgrounds. That was the other thing that bugged her about Fairy Fortune. Sometimes she couldn't be bothered with problems. And even when she could, that chirpy voice grated on the nerves after a while.

"Hey, you look great!" Tad greeted her as she descended the curving staircase. "I was just telling your mom I hoped you'd want to run over to the car lot with me."

"Oh, uh—sure," Bren replied with an uncertain smile. The car lot struck her as an odd place for a first date.

"Okay then, let's go," Tad said. "Nice meeting you, Mrs. Mickler." He opened the front door and ushered Bren through.

Outside, he held open the door of the blue van while she climbed into the passenger seat. All the way to the Thrifty Car

Lot, he talked about some "honey" of a car he had his eye on. Bren listened, wondering why guys talked about cars as though they were female. But then she remembered that Maya called her vintage Beetle Mr. Beep and smiled.

"What are you smiling about?" Tad asked, catching her eye in the rearview mirror. "That was definitely a Mona Lisa smile I saw just now. You know something else I ought to know about the future?"

"Nope. You know everything I know," she replied as he turned into the Thrifty Lot.

Red, white, and blue plastic triangles strung on overhead lines snapped and flapped in the breeze as she jumped out of the van, squinting in the harsh glare of the noon sun. A sea of used cars stretched over half a city block, but Tad made his way through them to the very back of the lot. He stopped in front of an aging car the exact shade of red as her knit top.

"What did I tell you—isn't she a beauty?" he asked, looking at the pile of metal as though he'd personally assembled it. "Nineteen-ninety-five Ford Thunderbird. Two-door LX. V-six engine. Seventy-six thousand miles."

Bren stared at the car. Seventy-six thousand miles seemed extreme, but what she knew about used cars would fit into the lid of an eye shadow square with room to spare. "Nice," she agreed

Tad sighed and crossed his arms. "Problem is, I gotta get this price down. I've got a good-sized down payment and a job, but the bank won't lend me more than four grand even with my parents' signatures. I need the dealer to come down at least twelve hundred dollars. Think it's going to happen?" He smiled that warm, honeyed smile that turned her knees to Gummi Worms. "Am I going to get my heart's desire?"

An electrical jolt zinged through her. *Heart's desire.* He hadn't been talking about her at all—he'd been talking about this dumb rattletrap of a car! A wave of disappointment crashed over her head.

"I—I don't know. I think so."

"I see you're back!" a voice called from behind them.

Bren turned as a young sales clerk in a white short-sleeved shirt and flapping tie came over to join them. "Sure is a beauty. I knew she'd get you back here for a second look." He patted a front fender and gave them a smarmy grin.

Bren felt herself recoil, but Tad patted the car's fender too. "I'm ready to buy," he told the salesperson. "But it's like I told you before, I need to get the price down."

The man mopped his sweating brow with the back of his arm and shook his head. "Can't do it," he said. "You know I already took that offer to my manager, and he nixed it. Best I can do is eight hundred."

"Awwww, man!" Tad groaned. "Where am I going to find another four hundred bucks before you sell this thing?"

"Sorry, buddy," the guy said. Already his eyes were scanning the lot, looking for a hotter prospect. He found one and made a beeline for her.

"So much for *that* prediction," Tad said as he and Bren walked back to the van. "I was so sure . . ."

Bren's mind hop-scotched back and forth between her disappointment over his heart's desire and the apparent wrongness of her prediction. She couldn't afford to let him down now. If she came up with too many wrong answers, he might not stick around long enough to get to know her. "Maybe it will still work out," she ventured. "Sometimes things work out later."

Tad shrugged and opened the van door for her. "Yeah, maybe," he muttered, not sounding convinced. His blue funk proved as contagious as the Asian flu. By the time he dropped her off at the fair, Bren felt as though *she* were the one who couldn't afford the car.

"Bren! There you are!" Nicole Johnson, one of junior varsity cheerleaders, greeted her at the booth. "You know that fortune you gave me yesterday? What a bust! You said I was going to be invited to the Gnosh before the game and so far, nothing has happened."

Bren sat down behind the computer and switched it on. She felt like zapping the astrology site into the ozone layer. "Hey, I only read them—I don't make them up," she replied. Her voice was cool, but inside she felt like dynamite had erupted somewhere near her solar plexus. What if Maya was right and astrology really *was* a stupid made-up thing? What would happen to business then? More important, what would happen to *her* if she had to start being in charge of decision making again?

A tall striking redhead with a smattering of freckles against skin as pale and flawless as porcelain sauntered over to the booth.

"I hear you guys do fortunes," she said. "Think you could do mine?" She pushed her long, impossibly thick hair behind one ear and waved a dollar bill. "I'm an Aquarius."

Bren pulled herself together. "Sure. Just give me a minute to get over to the site." She hit the Internet icon, clicked on the Favorites tab at the top of the screen, and selected the astrology site from the pull-down menu. While she worked the redhead carried on a conversation.

"You look familiar. You a cheerleader?" she asked.

Well, *duh*, Bren wanted to bark. She was sitting in the cheerleading booth trying to earn money for cheerleading uniforms. But she just nodded and waited for the site to load.

"I thought so. I saw you at games last year. I'm a cheerleader too. For Lakeland."

Lakeland. Tad's school. Bren sat up a little straighter and checked the girl out. Did she dare ask if she knew him? Better not. She probably did, but it wouldn't be a great idea to have her tell Tad that some lovesick cheerleader from Edgewood was asking about him.

"Okay, here you go," she said instead. "Aquarius. 'Romance takes center stage today. Your true love is faithful to you alone.'"

The redhead gave a little yelp of pleasure, reached in the pocket of her jean shorts, and tossed Bren another dollar. "Here! What you just said was worth every penny and then some!"

Bren took the bonus money and started to say thanks, then thought of something. "Want to double check?" she asked.

"Huh?" The redhead had started to turn away, but the question brought her back. "What do you mean?"

Bren reached to the ground for her tote bag and slowly extracted Fairy Fortune. "This is a fortune-telling ball," she explained. "You ask it a question, and it gives you a yes or no answer. Since you paid an extra dollar, you might as well give it a try."

The redhead looked at the ball like she wasn't sure whether to keep the prize behind Door Number One, or risk everything for Door Number Two. "Welllllll," she said slowly. "I guess I could. Okay. Ask it if what you told me before is true."

Bren picked up Fairy Fortune and asked, "Is this girl's true love going to remain faithful to her alone?"

"The answer cannot be anything but yes," the sugary voice responded.

"Oh! That is sooooooo cool!" the redhead squealed. "Thanks! I'll send my friends over. They're going to love this."

For the rest of the afternoon Bren kept one eye on business and the other on the door, praying that Tad would walk through, flash his slow, sweet smile, and ask her to join him at Lakeland's dance after the game. It didn't happen. And it didn't happen the next day either. A dentist appointment and cheerleading practice translated into zero time for her to be at the fair.

By the time Bren showed up at school for cheerleading practice, she was incapable of uttering a sentence anyone could understand. The dentist had filled a cavity, and her mouth was still numb from the shot of Novocain. The last thing she wanted to do was jump around hollering, "Push 'em back! Push 'em back! Way back!"

"Hi, Bren," Nicole greeted her as she walked out to the grass next to the parking lot where the cheerleaders gathered. "You still doing fortunes at the fair? Mine *still* hasn't worked out. You specifically said I was going to get asked to go to the Gnosh Friday night before the game, and so far nothing."

"Hey, that's right!" a varsity girl named Jen Parenti exclaimed. "What happened to that feeling of peace and calm I was supposed to get? My boyfriend and I got in a fight, and now he's not even going to the dance."

Bren waved them away. "I don't know anyshing about it," she slurped. "I jusht read whatsh online."

Jen giggled. "What's the matter with you? You sound like Porky Pig!"

Bren winced. Pigs. Jason. The dance was only a few days away and they would be going together. Ever since the disastrous trip to the used car lot, she hadn't even thought of it. "Dentisht," she explained, pointing to her mouth.

"Oh, that's funny," Jen giggled. "But I still think those predictions are off the mark. If the money weren't going to get us uniforms, I'd ask for a refund."

Suzanne jumped up from where she'd been sitting under a tree and rushed to Bren's defense. "That's not fair! Bren saved us from disaster. Without the fortunes, there wouldn't be a chance of getting new uniforms. And anyway . . ." She paused to smile at Bren. "My fortune was great, and I just know it's going to come true. I can feel it in my bones."

Bren returned the smile. "Thanks Suzanne. I've been right a lot of times. You could ask my new boyfriend. I predicted he would win big at the fair, and he won a huge bear at the ring tossh."

As soon as the words were out of her mouth, Bren regretted them. She'd actually called Tad her boyfriend! What if somebody knew somebody who knew him? One trip to the used car lot wasn't exactly the equivalent of dinner and a movie.

Ms. Malarkey, the cheerleading advisor, blew her whistle. "Come on girls! Line up please! We're in countdown mode here! Let's start with the train cheer."

The girls wandered away to take their marks in the grass, and Bren followed, fighting down a rising panic.

"Bang! Bang! Choo-choo train! Come on Edgewood, do your than!" Bren yelled the words and went through the motions on autopilot.

"Get it! Get it! Got it! Got it! HUH! And let it roll!" the cheerleaders finished.

Bren danced a dip to the side and made the motion of waves with her hand, wondering whether anybody had noticed what she'd said about Tad being her boyfriend.

"Good Bren!" Ms. Malarkey called. "Very good! Okay. I want to see the pyramid. Bren, you're on top."

A soft rumble of voices reacted, but Bren ignored them and climbed up two rows of crouching girls to pose. The top of the pyramid was highly prized, but right then she felt like a hood ornament on one of the land barges in the Thrifty Lot.

"Thanks a bunch, Bren," Suzanne muttered below her.

"Huh?" Bren wobbled and nearly fell.

"You know perfectly well what I mean!" Suzanne hissed. "Look who came out on top!"

Zap! The worry about Tad pulverized. Suzanne had obviously decided that "you'll come out on top" meant that she'd be at the top of the pyramid for Friday's game! Bren wobbled again and windmilled her arms. If two girls hadn't grabbed her ankles, there would have been at least three one-dimensional cheerleaders below her.

After practice, she apologized to Suzanne. "I really didn't know I'd get picked, Suzanne," she slurped. "What were the chanses of her choosing a klutz like me?"

Suzanne tossed her a dirty look and stalked to the parking lot.

"Don't let her bug you, Bren," Jen consoled her. "She's just jealous."

Of course Suzanne was jealous. Anyone could see *that*. But the problem wasn't just envy. It was that Suzanne thought Bren had done it to be mean. Bren sighed and headed to the parking lot where her mother sat waiting in her dark green SUV. She yanked open the passenger door and threw herself in the front seat.

"This is all shush a mesh," she wailed. She needed sympathy. Lots of sympathy. And maybe some vanilla ice cream in a chocolate shell.

"I'm sorry."

Bren looked at the person behind the wheel and screamed. The vehicle was a green SUV all right. But the driver was not her mother.

She'd climbed into a strange car next to somebody's father!

chapter.8

Bren stared at her computer screen and thought about the problem with Suzanne. After her parents had enjoyed a good laugh at what would go down in family legend as the Great Car Catastrophe, and she'd drowned her embarrassment in ice cream, she'd realized something. The palm reader had been right—she'd achieved success in cheerleading!

But Suzanne's prediction about coming out on top had sounded like *she'd* be the one at the top of the pyramid. Tad wasn't getting his heart's desire, Nicole hadn't been asked to the Gnosh, and Jen had had a fight with her boyfriend.

On the other hand, Tad had won big at the fair only moments after she'd predicted it. So many hits and misses made her head spin. Listlessly, she clicked over to the astrology site and checked her horoscope.

To make wonders happen, you must be willing to help the process.

Bren read the words in disbelief. Two clicks of the mouse and—*whammo!*—the perfect answer had appeared on the screen like magic. It wasn't the predictions that were the problem—it was her own lack of effort.

All this time she'd thought you just had to sit back and wait for stuff to happen when, clearly, fate required a sharp nudge in the ribs with a well-aimed elbow. It was so reassuring, she switched off her computer and went downstairs to watch a video with her dad. He'd picked up *Snow Day* on his way home from the hospital.

The next morning Bren begged Maya for a ride to the library on the pretext of needing to check the Cliff's Notes for *Pride and Prejudice*, the first book she'd finished for summer reading. She hated lying, but if Maya knew where she was really going, an argument was guaranteed.

As soon as Mr. Beep roared out of sight, Bren flew down the library steps and headed for the Thrifty Car Lot. The four-block walk was like plowing through a steam bath, but she trudged on, filled with resolve. Somehow she would get that price down on Tad's car.

At the lot, she wended her way through the sea of cars to the back where the red Ford gleamed like a metallic candy apple.

Bren crossed her arms and studied it as though she were a potential buyer. She patted the fender the way Tad had and gingerly kicked the front tire. Almost instantly, the same salesperson they'd talked to the day before made his way over to her.

"Hey there!" he greeted her. "Didn't I see you here yesterday?"

Bren nodded, grateful that the glare had required sunglasses. The trick to successful car negotiation, she knew, was not to seem too eager or desperate.

The salesman laughed, displaying a mouthful of crooked yellowed teeth. "Hah! I get it. The boyfriend couldn't afford it, so you thought you'd snatch it up for yourself. Smart girl. Of course you'll need a co-signer, but something tells me we can make this work." His gaze took in her expensive clothes and leather Coach bag.

"Mmmmmmm . . ." Bren said in her most noncommittal tone. "I don't know. It seems to me that Tad's right. You have this baby priced a little high considering the mileage." She cringed a little at calling a car "baby," but that's the kind of things guys said. Sometimes you just had to grit your teeth and talk the talk.

"You're kidding, right?" the salesman hooted. "That mileage is nothing. These days a car can go two-hundred thousand miles easy."

Bren frowned. She had no idea whether that was true, but the salesman clearly believed it. She decided to try another tact. "Well, maybe so," she conceded. "But you have to admit that the thing's been here awhile. I don't exactly see people lined up to buy it." She arched her eyebrows over the top of the sunglasses and stared at him.

"No, not this minute," he agreed. "But I got a guy supposed to come in tonight with his wife. They're probably bringing a down payment. If you want it, you better act fast. It won't be here tomorrow."

Bren looked at the car and fought a swell of panic. She had only one more ploy. "Hmmmmm. I think I'll pass," she said, lowering her voice to minus ten Fahrenheit. She shrugged and walked away without looking back.

This was where he was supposed to call her back to renegotiate, she thought as she squeezed through the tightly packed cars to the street. Unfortunately, they must not have told him that part at car-selling school.

Out on the sidewalk, she suddenly felt exhausted. Now what? She couldn't ask her friends for help. Nobody had that kind of money or even any connections in the car business. Besides, they all thought Tad was three sandwiches short of a picnic with all his psychic-babble.

That left only one person she could ask for help. Her dad. She picked up her pace and hurried to the library, up the steps, and into the lobby to the pay phone. Quickly, she dropped some coins in the slot and checked her watch. With any luck he'd have seen his last morning patient but not yet left for lunch.

"Dr. Mickler," he said on the third ring.

"Daddy? Hi. Uh—I was wondering if you could help me with something."

"What is it, sweetheart? Is something wrong?" The concern in his voice zoomed through the fiber-optic lines.

"No, well, not exactly." Bren clutched the receiver with a sweaty hand and took a deep breath. "The thing is, I have this friend, Tad, and he needs a car loan. Not for the whole amount or anything—he has a bank loan already for most of it. But the problem is, we can't get the price down and the bank won't come up in what they're willing to lend and—well—I thought maybe you could give him a loan. He has a job, and he's really trustworthy, and you could make money off the interest and . . ." She was babbling. She realized it, stopped, and held her breath.

"Honey, I know you want to help your friend . . ."

He didn't have to say any more. The answer was fugetaboutit. Bren listened while he explained the folly of lending money to people you hardly knew, especially when they weren't completely bank approved, and then she hung up the phone. She had no more ideas. Tad was not going to get his heart's desire. Period.

At home she logged on to the daily chat with little enthusiasm.

nycbutterfly: where have U been? I am dying 2 make an announcement
chicChick: I was at the library. u took me there, remember? Wazzup?
nycbutterfly: Promise not 2 laff U guys. but I want 2 take

gymnastics. I know I'm old 2 start, but it's weird. it's
like I have a cosmic pull 2ward it.

Bren did a double take. Cosmic pull? Since when did Maya
run around saying things like cosmic pull?

faithful1: No way! U can't do that. U could get hurt. What
happens 2 the swim team THEN? And what's with this
cosmic stuff? Not U 2?

rembrandt: I think Maya should do what she wants. wish
I could. But the Art Czar won't let me. he insists I
work on color. Says my colors R 2 muddy. Muddy! I
don't even know whether 2 believe him. what do U
think, Bren?

Bren's mouth dropped open. Was Jamie asking for her opinion about Garrett Lindstrom or hinting that she might want her
horoscope read after all?

chicChick: How would I know?

rembrandt: because U have UR wagon hitched to the
stars!

faithful1: ACK!

TX2step: double ACK! I don't want 2 talk about this junk.
I'm worried about my mom. She's had strep and I'm
wondering if it's OK for her 2 travel so far 2 visit me

Bren felt a surge of excitement. Could it be that Alex was pretending she still thought astrology was bogus but actually wanted a reading? It would be so like her not to be able to admit she was wrong.

Maybe all of them—except Amber—were becoming more open-minded now that they had problems of their own. Bren reached over and picked up Fairy Fortune from the shelf above her desk and closed her eyes.

"Should Alex's mother make the trip from Texas?" she asked.

"I'm sorry, but the answer is no. Definitely no," chirped the fairy.

Startled, Bren opened her eyes. She'd been so sure the answer would be yes. Alex would be disappointed—it had been a long time since she'd seen her mom. Just to be sure, she asked the ball a second time. The answer was still no.

chicChick: I know how much U want UR mom 2 come, but she shouldn't do it 2step. Tell her 2 wait a week.
TX2step: ACK! R U sure?

Bren hesitated.

chicChick: Yes.

By the time she logged off, Bren felt recharged. Her friends were definitely coming around—even if they wouldn't admit it.

As for the problem with Tad, maybe she'd started too big. Maybe she needed to build up to his car crisis by nudging the easy problems first. Almost immediately, she hit on ideas to help all the cheerleaders, including Suzanne. In fact, Suzanne's was the cleverest nudge of all.

The next morning she waited outside the door of the cow barn at the fairgrounds. It was the last day of the fair, and Jamie had said that Michael Kellerman, Jen's boyfriend, had made a deal on his prize steer and would be there to hand it over to its new owner. She watched him unfold his lanky body from the inside of a souped-up white pickup perched on tires as big as kiddy pools.

"Hey Michael! Can I talk to you a minute?" she hollered.

He looked up, surprised, then made his way over to her. "What can I do for you?" he asked, giving her an appraising glance. Kellerman played first string basketball, but Bren didn't think he was all that cute. For one thing, he had a smile that made her feel like she needed a shower.

"I know you and Jen had a fight," she began, biting her lip. Now that she was actually meddling, she felt uneasy. "Um, the thing is she feels really bad. The dance is coming up pretty soon, of course, but what she really feels bad about is you, and she wishes that . . . but of course she doesn't know I'm talking to you so . . . you know. I mean I wish you wouldn't . . ." She was babbling again. She stopped and waited for a reaction.

He grinned and reached past her to slide open the barn door. "Huh," he said. "Cool."

Bren stared after him as he walked into the dim, smelly interior, alive with the sound of mooing cows. She wasn't sure if he was glad to know Jen wanted to make up, or was just tickled to hear that she was in a snit. The other nudges would be much easier, she promised herself, because her friends would make them happen.

Bren cornered Amber next at her church's snow-cone stand. "You have to help me!" she pleaded, beginning Nudge B. "You know Suzanne Kennedy—the cheerleader? Well, she wants to write something for the school paper. For that column, 'On Top of Edgewood.'" She couldn't resist a giggle at her own inventiveness. The column's title had popped into her head just when she'd been casting around for something that Suzanne would immediately equate with her fortune.

Suzanne was in Honors English, so she was more than capable of producing a good column. It was perfect. Better than perfect because the next time Suzanne whined about not being on the top of the pyramid, it would be a cinch to explain that the prediction hadn't been *about* cheerleading.

"Suzanne Kennedy?" Amber frowned. "I never heard her express any interest in the paper. Yeah, I suppose I could ask her. What's she want to write about?"

Bren shrugged. "I don't know. Just don't let on I said anything. Pretend you're asking her out of the blue. She'll be so excited. She's—uh—had some disappointments lately."

Amber nodded. "Okay, I guess I could. Sure. Why not?"

Bren headed next to the arts building where Jamie was taking her turn painting while people watched. Every year the interest in watching artists at work grew in popularity at the fair. There was no crowd this early though, so she could corner her friend and get on with Nudge C while she was on a roll. Bren flopped down in the chair Jamie would occupy later and let out a sigh.

"What's the matter?" Jamie asked, looking up from the rickety easel she was trying to assemble.

"Nothing. I just feel bad for Nicole Johnson, that little freshman cheerleader on J.V.," Bren replied.

Jamie gave one of the easel's wooden legs a hard kick. "Really? What happened to her?"

Bren shrugged. She felt sort of manipulative, but she reminded herself that it was for a good cause. "Oh, it's not a big deal. Unless you're a freshman," she added. "Poor thing's never been asked to go to the Gnosh, and she really wants to go. You know what a kick that is when you start high school and start hanging there with your friends."

Jamie looked baffled. "So ask her to join us before the game Friday. What's the problem?"

"No problem," Bren replied. "I just thought maybe you could ask her. If I do, it would look like pity. I'm the one she confessed to, after all."

Jamie nodded. "Sure," she agreed. "That makes sense. I'll do it today. I'll get Morgan and Alex to invite her too. Consider it done." She dragged the easel near a sunny window.

Bren wandered back to the Industry Expo building. Maya and Morgan should be there, doing their stint manning their dad's jukebox and handing out flyers about the Gnosh.

Every year on the last day of the fair, Mr. Cross trucked in a vintage Wurlitzer jukebox and played 50s hits. *Peggy Sue* was already blaring out of the neon-lit machine as Bren entered the building. It was the song that little piggy Peggy Sue had been named for. Bren thought about how nice Jason had been that afternoon and felt a tinge of guilt about the upcoming dance.

Maya and Morgan stood right by the door, their hands full of bubble-gum pink flyers. "Good morning ladies!" Bren greeted them. She grabbed Morgan by the hand and twirled her around to the music.

"You sure are cheerful," Maya said, sounding anything *but*.

Bren dropped Morgan's hand and studied Maya. "What's the matter? You look like you lost your best buddy."

Maya punched another selection as *Peggy Sue* ended. "I can't get in a gymnastics class," she said glumly. "The one at the racquet club requires membership and my dad hit the roof over the six hundred dollar initiation fee. And the one at Dance On! is full. So it looks like it's over. At least for now."

Bren shook her head. "No, it's not. I read your horoscope this morning. In fact, I cut it out of the paper for you." She rummaged around in her tote bag until she found the scrap of newsprint. "Listen to what it says. 'Answers are found behind the scenes. What seemed to be a defeat will boomerang in your favor.' Isn't that wild?"

Maya perked up a little, then slumped against the side of the Wurlitzer. "Well, yeah, if it were true," she said. "But I can't imagine what could happen to change it. They have a waiting list at Dance On! that's fifteen people long."

"Just wait and see," Bren advised. She could hardly contain her glee. This was so fixable it was like stacking blocks in nursery school. She danced with Morgan to *Rock around the Clock*, then made an excuse about needing to meet someone and dashed for the pay phone. After yesterday's refusal to loan money to Tad, she knew her father would be reluctant to say no to her again.

His secretary buzzed her right over to his office. "Hi honey," Dr. Mickler said when he heard her voice. "No more car loans I hope."

Bren giggled. "Nope, not today. This is for Maya. Don't you do the physicals for that dance school Dance On!?"

"As a matter of fact, I do," he replied. "Maya need one?"

"Hopefully," Bren said. "But first she needs to get in. They're full to the rafters for gymnastics. Do you think there's any way you could—uh—maybe see if . . ."

"Consider it done, sweetie. I'll do my best," he cut in. "I'm pretty good friends with Sonja Goldstone, the owner."

Bren hung up the phone, fighting an urge to twirl down the

midway like a five-year-old on a sugar high. If it could be done, it would be. And she had a hunch it could.

That evening, she logged on to the Internet a half-hour before the scheduled chat and clicked over to TodaysGirls.com to see if anyone else was early. No one was, but Amber had posted a new Thought for the Day.

God is not a God of confusion, but a God of peace. (1 Corinthians 14:33)

When life seems overwhelming and the future looks scary, isn't it great the way we can look to God? It's like--what else do we need?

Bren let out a huge sigh. Amber was still on her kick about fortune-telling. She clicked over to www.snap.com and typed "used cars" in the box at the top of the screen. She had no idea how you bought something as big as a car over the Internet, but she'd heard it was possible.

She clicked on the first site listed and right away, it popped on her screen offering two search options—by model or by price. She decided to search by model. She scrolled down the menu until she came to Ford Thunderbird and clicked. Then she entered her zip code and clicked *Go*. As it loaded, she realized the way it worked was that you indicated what you were looking for, and it put you in touch with dealers in your own area who had it.

When the page loaded, Bren scanned the dozen listings. All were for the Thunderbird 2 door LX, but there was only one that listed both the right year and the right color. She clicked it and read the dealer's description, half afraid it was the car Tad had already been haggling over. Her eyes took in the key words—leather seats, power windows, cruise control, CD player—and she felt her excitement build. It wasn't. There were two problems, but neither was insurmountable. The important thing was that the price was right.

The car had twenty thousand more miles than the other one, but cars these days went to 200,000 miles easy. That's what the guy at Thrifty had said. And the fact that the dealer was 90 miles away was no biggie either. Sometimes to get what you wanted you had to work for it, Bren decided.

She printed the page for herself and sent the dealership an e-mail:

Please send this ad to the following e-mail address. This is a very interested and qualified buyer. But it's a surprise, so please don't mention that the address was forwarded. Thank you.

She hit *Send* and clicked over to TodayGirls.com again. If she could pull this off, Tad Campbell would get his heart's desire. Even better, Bren Mickler would get hers.

Bren woke at five-thirty A.M. to a shrieking alarm. After three months of sleeping late, it felt weird to rise with the birds. Today was the first day of school, and Coach had notified the swim team that there was nothing like practice on the first day to get the season off to a "swimming" start. Bren shook her head at the lame joke, grabbed her swimsuit, and met her mom in the kitchen for a ride to school.

"Good morning, sleepyhead," Mrs. Mickler chirped in that too-cheery morning voice that made Bren's teeth hurt.

Bren gave her a wan wave and went out to the garage. She felt like she'd been run over by a water buffalo. Ten minutes later she dragged into the locker room still rubbing sleep from her eyes.

"Hey Bren," Amber greeted her. "You're sure moving slow this morning. We were wondering if you were going to show up."

Alex stood at the mirror braiding her long russet hair. "Yeah. I just said that maybe you'd predicted the outcome of the first meet and figured there was no point in practicing." She laughed and turned to Maya. "Didn't I just say that?"

Maya turned away from the mirror where she'd been rubbing moisturizer on her face. "Hey, give the girl a break, will you? I think she's smarter than we give her credit for."

Bren's tiredness evaporated. "Huh?" She stared at Maya. "What do you mean?"

"I mean," Maya said, putting the cap back on the tube of moisturizer, "that I got the weirdest e-mail from Dance On! yesterday. It said that if I still want to be in the gymnastics class, all I have to do is call. They even said I don't need a new physical if I already have one for school sports, which of course I do. So I can start tomorrow. I never saw it until late though because Morgan and I stayed at the fair to watch the closing fireworks. So I still have to call them today, but it looks like it's in the bag. Isn't that the coolest? I was sixteenth on the list!"

Alex stopped braiding and looked at Maya with eyes the size of golf balls. "Are you kidding? How could that be? That's too weird."

Maya shrugged and grinned at Bren. "I have no clue, but I'm a happy girl!"

Bren could hardly contain her glee as she changed into her suit. Things were starting to look up. If Maya was this happy over gymnastics, Tad would be over the moon when he got the car ad. She dressed quickly and rejoined her friends at the pool. They were still buzzing about Maya's gymnastics class.

"This is nuts, Maya. You could get hurt," Amber said for the zillionth time. "Gymnastics is a dangerous sport. Those professionals you see have been doing it for years—since they were tiny."

Coach Short came over to the group just after Bren joined them. "Gymnastics?" he asked. "Did I hear something about one of you taking gymnastics?"

"Maya's signing up for classes at Dance On!" Alex informed him.

Coach tapped his clipboard with his pen. "Is that true, Maya?"

Maya gave Alex an annoyed look and nodded. "Yes, I've thought it would be fun to try it out."

"Well, I don't approve at all," Coach said giving her what Bren always called his Wise Man stare. "All it would take is one injury, and the swim team's in jeopardy. I can't stop you of course, but I am bound to tell you that this is a crazy idea—if not an irresponsible one."

Maya blinked in surprise at the word irresponsible but didn't say anything.

"Maya's not being irresponsible," Alex defended her. "Bren told her her horoscope said it would be okay."

Coach let out a cross between a disbelieving yelp and a strangled snort. "Horoscopes? Now I've truly heard it all. Bren, don't tell me you believe that nonsense?"

Bren shrugged and stared at the floor.

"I certainly hope none of you are foolish enough to think that astrology holds the answers to anything. The truth is . . ." Coach stopped and shook his head. "You get the picture. Now come on, let's get in gear."

Bren jumped into the pool, glad to hide her embarrassment in six feet of water. But by the time practice was over and she was dressed and in the hall collecting compliments, Coach Short had vanished from her thoughts like the picture on a TV screen when you zap the off button.

Suzanne rushed over and touched her arm. "Maybe your fortune-telling idea wasn't a total flop," she said. "We counted the money last night, and we made a bundle. The uniforms are guaranteed."

"Hey, Bren, my fortune came true! Thanks a bunch," another girl called as she passed.

Bren smiled and walked to her first class. She was so busy basking in the glow of success that she never noticed Jason Hersh until he was walking alongside her.

"Hi, stranger," he said. "I've tried to call you, but you're never home. My sister wanted you to help her with the pigs."

Bren forced herself to stay calm. Somehow she had to get out of this conversation before the subject of the dance came up. She didn't want to go with him, but she didn't know how to say so.

She also knew he'd called a lot. Every night her machine had blinked with his many messages. "I know," she apologized. "I'm sorry. I was at the fair practically nonstop. You know how that is. Listen, could you maybe do me a favor?"

"Sure," Jason replied.

Bren's brain raced. "You know Michael Kellerman, right? On the basketball team? Dates Jen Parenti? I was wondering if you could talk with him about Jen. They had this fight, and Jen is just devastated. I talked to him already, but I think it would hold more weight coming from a guy."

For all she knew, Jen and Michael had made up already, but she was desperate to keep him from bringing up the dance. "Oops, this is my class. Gotta go! Talk to him, okay?"

She ducked into the biology lab and breathed a sigh of relief when he didn't follow her. As soon as she saw him turn the corner she headed off to her real class.

All morning Bren received compliments, plus dozens of requests for more predictions. Someone even suggested they petition the school to start an Astrology Club and name her president.

Even when the math teacher overheard her whispering a prediction to the guy in front of her and said in front of the whole class, "Ms. Mickler, I predict you will fail this class if you don't start paying attention," she laughed it off.

At lunch she offered her friends updates on their futures. She felt strong and sure of herself—and even a little reckless. "Alex, you definitely should not have your mother traveling in her weakened condition. And Maya gymnastics is absolutely right for you."

Maya dropped her tuna sandwich and jumped to her feet. "Oh! Thanks for reminding me!" she exclaimed. "I forgot to call Dance On! You guys had me believing it was a done deal. I'll be right back." She grabbed her purse, left her lunch on the table, and dashed to the pay phones in the Commons.

"Now Jamie," Bren said. She slowly peeled a banana and thought about how to word what she had to say so Jamie wouldn't go ballistic. Jamie's problem with Garrett Lindstrom was the only one she had actually checked last night. The psychic site on the Internet and Fairy Fortune had both been in agreement. "I think this seminar has really been hard on you," she said carefully.

Jamie nodded. "You don't know the half of it."

Bren reached across the table and patted her friend's hand. "I do know, Jamie. You've been so stressed and upset, and I hate seeing you like that. You need to ditch this thing. Garrett Lindstrom is not worth it. And that's not just me talking either," she added. "Though it *is* what I think too." She took a bite of banana and steeled herself in case Jamie got on her high horse about astrology again.

"Thanks, Bren," Jamie said. "You're right. I know it. I think I need to let it go and maybe see what kind of classes the museum offers over the winter. They always have stuff."

Bren glanced at Amber. Her face was redder than an overripe tomato. She started to say something but was stopped by Maya, who bounded into the lunchroom and flopped into her seat. "I'm in!" she announced. "I got the last spot! Oh, I'm so excited! I don't know how I'm going to wait till tomorrow. Amber will you run to the mall with me tonight and help me pick out a leotard?"

The color in Amber's face deepened to cranberry. "No! I won't! Maya, this is the most selfish thing you've ever done!" she cried. "I can't believe you'd leave the entire swim team hanging out on a limb just so you can pretend you're Shannon Miller! Coach is right—you're irresponsible!"

The explosion silenced the table. Everyone stared at Amber with their mouths hanging open. Although she never had trouble expressing an opinion, Amber Thomas certainly wasn't given to outbursts.

"I'm sorry you feel that way," Maya replied in a voice dripping icicles. "But this really isn't any of your business. The last time I checked *I* was in charge of what I did with my spare time—not you or Coach Short."

"Please don't fight you guys!" Jamie pleaded.

Amber jerked her chair back and jumped to her feet. "Don't worry!" she shot back. "I'm not fighting with anybody because I'm not talking to any of you! You're all jumping on the bandwagon with this astrology thing, and I'm sick of it!"

Jamie, Bren, and Maya gaped in disbelief as Amber picked up her lunch tray and stormed across the room to another table.

chapter.10

"**B**ren Mickler, you have some nerve!" Suzanne Kennedy shouted as Bren walked across the grass to where the cheerleaders waited to begin their last practice before the game. She was so angry she was shaking. "How dare you get Amber Thomas to ask me to write for the school paper? What do you think I am—stupid? 'On Top of Edgewood'? Ha-ha. Very funny."

Bren gaped at Suzanne's angry, contorted face. She'd asked Amber not to tell Suzanne it had been her idea. But clearly she'd spilled the beans just to get even.

"What are you talking about?" she asked, stalling for time. Everyone was watching, including some of the kids standing around waiting for rides after other practices.

Suzanne snorted. "Oh, don't give me that innocent act. I know very well that you asked Amber to ask me to write for the paper just so you could look good. Your prediction didn't work out about cheerleading, so you had to cover your tracks."

A hot flush crept up Bren's neck. Suzanne was right. She'd done exactly that. But when she'd decided to do it, it had seemed innocent, not mean-spirited the way it sounded now.

"What makes you think I'd do something to hurt you?" Bren asked, still stalling. She looked around, praying someone would come to her defense, but everyone just stood by and watched.

"I just know you did, that's all," Suzanne said. "And I think it's mean."

"Get in line girls! No time to waste! Come on—move it! Let's go!" Ms. Malarkey called, coming across the parking lot waving her arms.

Bren mentally thanked her for the save as she took her spot in the front row. She didn't know which hurt most—what Suzanne had said to her, or the fact that Amber had betrayed her.

She knew Amber was mad, but anger was one thing and breaking a promise just to get even was something else. All during practice, she jumped, screamed, flipped, and even climbed on the pyramid, but her heart felt almost too heavy to lug around.

"Bren, can I talk with you a minute?" Ms. Malarkey asked after dismissal.

Bren nodded. She was glad to have a chance to talk to the coach because somewhere in the middle of "Bang! Bang! Choo-choo Train" she'd reached a decision.

"What's the matter with you today? You're way off the mark. You aren't getting sick are you?" Ms. Malarkey asked. "Is something wrong?"

Just my whole life, Bren thought, but she shook her head no. "Ms. Malarkey, I've been thinking about the pyramid," she said slowly. "Do you think maybe Suzanne Kennedy could do the top instead of me? I feel really shaky up there. You know I'm not exactly a gazelle." She managed a small grin.

Ms. Malarky didn't smile back. "Suzanne's a little heavy to be on top," she said.

"I know," Bren agreed. "But she can do it, and she really wants it. I'm just not comfortable up there. Please?"

Ms. Malarkey gave her a long, appraising look before nodding. "Okay, but to make this work we're going to need another practice tomorrow before the game. I want to make sure she's okay up there. If not, you're it. You also need to call everyone and make arrangements for them to come early. Deal?"

"Deal." Bren said.

She walked across the grass to the sidewalk, glad that she'd called her mother earlier to say she was going to stop at the Gnosh and grab a burger for dinner and talk to Jamie.

The Gnosh wasn't busy when she came in, and Jamie was just about ready to go on break. Bren ordered a cheeseburger and her favorite onion rings, and Jamie brought them out and joined her in a booth with a bowl of soup.

"That was really big of you to give her the top of the pyramid,"

Jamie said after Bren spilled the story. "I know you never did it to be mean. You only want the best for everyone. Like me, for instance."

She slurped a spoonful of soup and said quietly, "I told Garrett Lindstrom I was quitting last night."

Bren's sandwich slipped from her hands, and she swallowed hard to get the last bite down her throat. All of a sudden, she wished she hadn't been so glib with the predictions. "What did he say?" she asked, swallowing again. Jamie looked bluer than the indigo shirt she was wearing.

She stirred the creamy soup and leaned on her elbow, looking sad. "Not much. Other than that he thought it was ungrateful of me to take a spot and then drop out. I don't think he cared beyond that."

"How do you feel?" Bren asked.

Jamie shrugged, "All right I guess. Relieved sort of." She sniffled.

Bren wanted to make sure Jamie was really all right. Had that been a teary, sad sniffle or just one brought on by the steamy soup? But Maya and Morgan came breezing through the door and crowded into the booth, shattering the opportunity.

"Are you guys going to the dance?" Morgan asked after Maya got them both Cokes. "Maya's not. I was, but now I don't know. Jared and I were supposed to go together like we always go to stuff, but he hasn't called me, and every time I call him his mom says he's not home. I don't know what's wrong."

Bren felt a stab of guilt but shook her head to rid herself of it. She had nothing to do with Jared and Morgan's relationship, she told herself. If they were on bad terms it was their own problem. Besides, Jared was probably just swamped with homework or something.

"What are we going to do about Amber?" Bren asked, changing the subject. She told Maya what had happened with Suzanne. "I think maybe Amber told her I set it up about her writing for the paper. She's mad at us all, and it would be a good way to get even."

"No way! No *way!*" Maya protested, slapping the tabletop for emphasis, then crossing her arms. "I know Amber's mad at all of us, but I know my girl well enough to know she'd never do something like that. Her word's sacred—even when she's ticked off. Trust me."

Bren considered it. Maya was Amber's best friend, but something told her Maya wasn't just defending her out of loyalty. She really meant it.

"I guess you're right," she agreed. "I suppose it wasn't all that hard to figure out. Hey, can you run me home?"

"Sure," Maya replied. "Let's hit it though. I have a quiz tomorrow."

As soon as Maya pulled into the driveway, Bren flew out of the car, into the house, and up the steps to her room with only a brief hello to her parents, who were playing Pictionary in the living room with their friends, the Wilsons.

It seemed like light years since she'd asked the dealership to forward the car ad to Tad. Maybe by now there would be a response. Bren booted up her computer, logged onto the Internet, and went over to Outlook Express. She checked her messages and watched hopefully as five whizzed by on the green bar at the top of the screen. None were from Tad.

For a moment, she stared at the screen feeling defeated. Then she hit *New Message,* retrieved Tad's e-mail address from her Address Book, and typed:

Hi, Just wondering if you heard any more about the car?
I still predict you're going to get your heart's desire! Write
me! Bren

She hit *Send* and closed her eyes, willing him to contact her. It had been such a long day. She deserved something good just for having gotten through it, she told herself. The phone at her elbow shrilled, causing her to jumped a foot in her chair.

"Hi, this is Bren," she said cheerily. She was a master at the quick-change thing. If fashion design didn't work out, she often thought she could make a great living on the stage.

"Finally! Are you always this difficult to get hold of? Makes it hard to have a relationship, you know?"

Jason Hersh. Bren felt the cheeseburger and onion rings she'd just eaten turn to stone in her stomach. Not only was she without an escape, but he'd actually used the "r" word.

"I've just been awfully busy," she managed. "Had cheerleading practice tonight."

"Oh, yeah. Right. I forgot," Jason said. "Listen, we never did figure out where to meet after the game. I don't know what you girls do after you leave the field."

Bren gulped. She checked her e-mail twice and considered her options.

"Bren? Are you there?"

"Yes, yes, I was just trying to think," Bren replied. She reached over and picked up Fairy Fortune and formulated a quick question in her head. *Should I go to the dance with Jason?*

"No, I do not believe so," came the response.

"What's that voice?" Jason asked. "Every time I call you anymore it sounds like somebody is right there next to the phone. Like a little kid or something."

Bren set the fortune ball down on the desk carefully. Her mouth felt dry as the wad of cotton on top of her vitamin bottle.

"Jason, I . . . I can't . . . I'm sorry . . . I don't . . ." She groped for words and stumbled over the few she found.

There was a pause. A looooooooong pause. Long enough to dial a phone number, heat a muffin in the microwave, or address an envelope.

"I get it," he said finally. "You're telling me our date's off."

Bren nodded, even though he couldn't see it. She felt like a rat. A big fat brown urban rat—the kind that were taking over New York City.

"I'm sorry, Jason," she said. "I feel so bad telling you this so late, but . . ." She thought frantically, trying to find something—anything—that would get her off the hook and spare his ego.

Just then an instant message popped up!

Tad!

"I'm sorry, Jason." A new firmness took over her voice. "I'm sure you can ask someone else. Listen, I have to run. I'll catch you tomorrow, okay?"

She hung up the phone.

chapter.11

Bren clicked into Instant Messenger like a small child at Christmas. This could be the reason Fortune Fairy had advised her to turn Jason down. She pictured Tad's honey smile as she read his first line:

linebacker: Hey, Stargazer. I think U have psychic powers!

Bren smiled to herself. He'd gotten the ad!

chicChick: What do U mean?
linebacker: I got my heart's desire just like U predicted!
   Weird how it happened 2. Got an e-mail ad out of the
   blue. Dealership was sort of far, but deal was 2 good 2
   pass up. U said it wouldn't B easy and U were right!

chicChick: Cool! When R you getting it?

linebacker: Already have it! I took the day off school, and my dad and I went. That's why I'm on here. Thought u'd want 2 see it.

Bren was so excited she could barely type.

chicChick: U bet I do! When?

linebacker: How about u meet me after the game tomorrow?

chicChick: Gr8! Parking lot ok? I will know ur car!

linebacker. Yeah--right. Gr8!

By the time they logged off, Bren was so jazzed she couldn't concentrate on anything but the thought of seeing Tad. Even an upcoming test on *Pride and Prejudice* couldn't keep her attention for more than two seconds.

Jane Austen's romances rocked even though they'd been written in Regency England, but they were just fiction. *Her* romance was real—or would be very soon, if things worked out the way she hoped they would.

There *was* one thing that sort of bothered her though. Tad hadn't mentioned either his dance or hers. He hadn't even suggested going to the Gnosh. But surely he didn't mean that they would look at the stupid car and go their separate ways.

Bren shoved it out of her mind and opened her closet. The

trick was to find a killer outfit to change into before she met him, she decided. She pulled out a pair of light gray pants, a lavender tank top, and a cute little matching lavender shrug.

The next morning, Bren arrived at school early and went off to the art room in search of Jamie who had volunteered to reorganize the supply closet before class. Bren poked her head in the door and found Jamie on her hands and knees stacking sheets of colored paper.

"Hi!" she called. "You almost done?" The look on Jamie's face stopped her cold. "What's wrong?"

"Nothing. Everything. I don't know," Jamie replied. She continued to stack paper by color, but the slump of her shoulders told it all. She was big-time depressed.

"Is this about the Art Czar?" Bren demanded. She came into the room and knelt down next to her friend in front of the huge metal cabinet. "You should be glad you're done with him!"

Jamie shrugged and placed the paper on the bottom shelf, then turned her attention to a plastic bucket filled with felt-tipped markers. Bren watched as one by one she uncapped them and tried them out to see if they still worked. "I think maybe I made a mistake," Jamie said finally. "At first I was relieved, but now I feel sort of sick."

Bren felt a stab of sickness herself but willed it away. "Don't be silly," she said firmly. "The guy was nuts. You said so yourself. It's not like he's the only opportunity you're ever going to get. Get *real!*"

Jamie put the cap on a brown marker and looked Bren squarely in the eye. "That's the problem," she said softly. "I *am* getting real. Which is why I know I blew an amazing opportunity."

Bren felt a rushing sensation, like her head was filling up with white noise. She swallowed hard and tried again. "I'm sorry you feel so bad," she said, groping for the right words to make Jamie okay with her decision. "But you know what it was doing to you, Jamie. It was killing you. He was so mean and critical . . ."

Bren stopped in mid-sentence. Jamie wasn't buying it.

All morning Jamie's sadness popped up in Bren's thoughts like spam in a computer mailbox. No matter how hard she tried to delete it, there it was again. By the time she went to lunch, she was praying Amber would have a Thought for the Day about being true to yourself or believing in the future. Anything that would help Jamie.

"Hi gang!" Bren greeted her friends at the table. She set down her chili dog and fries and slid into her seat. "Guess what?" she asked with forced cheerfulness. "Tad wants to meet me tonight after the game!"

"I thought Jason Hersh asked you out," Alex said, spreading grape jelly on a peanut butter sandwich.

Bren felt a stab of guilt. Jason. Why did she always keep forgetting about Jason? She registered one more tiny guilt twinge and brushed him aside. "He did. But I said no. I'm really not interested in him. Anyway, Tad got this new car, and he wants to show it to me. Keep your fingers crossed he either asks to come to our dance or asks me to go to his." She crossed the fingers on both hands and held them up.

Alex snorted. "Like that's gonna work," she muttered.

Bren ignored her. "Come on—be nice. I'm so excited you guys! He is so cute and so nice, and I know he likes me. I just wish he'd already made a plan for tonight. But I guess it doesn't matter. He's more of a casual sort of guy." She dipped a fry in a glob of ketchup and glanced over at Maya, who hadn't said a word. Something light brown poked out from under the cuff of Maya's long-sleeved white shirt.

"What's that?" Bren asked, pointing at it.

Maya unbuttoned the cuff of her shirt and held out her arm.

Bren's eyes popped. "Why are you wearing an elastic bandage?" she asked. A little quiver of fear formed in the pit of her stomach. Out of the corner of her eye she could see Amber sitting alone at a table near the door watching everything as she slowly peeled and ate an orange.

"First night at gymnastics, and already I got zapped," Maya replied. "It's not serious. I was trying to do a cartwheel and I sprained my wrist. Doc says it's no big deal, but Coach is livid. I'm off the team until further notice."

"Whaaaaaaaaaaat?" Bren sputtered. She jumped up from her seat. "He can't do that! He said himself he can't tell you not to do gymnastics. What does he think—that you did this on purpose, or what? This is soooooo unfair! I'm going to go talk to him."

"No you're not," Maya replied. She rebuttoned her sleeve and gave Bren a stern look. "I'm serious Bren. Let it be."

Bren sat back down. "But it isn't fair," she argued.

Maya shrugged.

"It wasn't all that fair to the team to risk an injury either," Alex remarked.

Bren steeled herself for another explosion, but none came. Maya continued to eat her lunch without a reply. It was obvious that on some level she agreed.

After lunch Bren walked to her next class alone. Thoughts of Maya and Jamie conflicted with the exhilaration of seeing Tad. And Jason hovered in the shadows of her mind like a cat burglar waiting to pounce.

"Hey Bren!" one of the football players yelled from across the hall. He was heading the opposite direction, but he wove across a river of moving bodies to get to her. "I wanted to ask you— who do you think is going to win tonight?"

Bren gave him a blank stare. She had no clue. From what Tad had said about defense, it wasn't likely to be Edgewood. The last thing she wanted to do was make a prediction about anything—especially without the Internet, the newspaper, or Fairy Fortune.

"Um—I think it looks good if Edgewood plays hard, and the team gives it all they've got," she said. It was lame. She knew it, but it was the best she could do. "I have to run, or I'll be late for class," she muttered, hurrying up the hall.

"Thanks Bren—you really *are* good!" the guy called behind her.

Bren ducked into Ms. Paris's English class and took her seat.

It would be funny if she weren't so stressed, she thought. She hadn't made any prediction at all—she'd just stated the obvious, and the guy had grabbed onto it like a lifeline. She dug in her bag for a pen and waited for Ms. Paris to hand out the test she had been too keyed-up to study for. Two thoughts about fortune-telling tried to make a connection in her brain—something about the guy in the hall and the palm reader at the fair.

"Ohhhhhhhhhh," the girl across the aisle groaned. "This test is unreal!"

The thought connection fizzled as Bren took her copy of the test from Ms. Paris. The girl across the aisle had nailed it. The test was a doozy, and Bren Mickler was staring down the bore of a solid D.

After English, she cornered Jamie as they were leaving the room.

"Forgot to tell you," she said. "I can't have dinner at the Gnosh tonight. I have cheerleading practice before the game. There's a change we have to practice, and everybody has to be there."

"Okay, whatever," Jamie said. "I don't even know if I'll go to the game. I'm definitely not doing the dance. I think maybe I'm going to tell Mr. Cross I'll work."

Bren looked at Jamie's sad face and felt sick all over again. "But there won't be all that much business," she argued. "Everybody will be at the dance."

"Not everybody," Jamie replied. "There's always a crowd that doesn't go. Besides, a lot of adults come in after the game. He'll be happy to have me work."

Bren didn't push it. Everything had gotten so complicated, and somehow it felt like it was her fault. But she hadn't really done anything. She'd just read the predictions, and everyone had believed them.

"Bren! Wait up!" Suzanne called. She hurried up to Bren clutching her books against her chest like a shield. "Do you want a ride to practice tonight?"

Bren did a double take. Jamie's problems and her own evaporated as she stared at the girl who only two days earlier had screamed at her at practice. "You're offering me a ride?" she asked faintly.

Suzanne nodded, her short dark hair wisped around her ears. "Yeah. I'm sorry I freaked. Ms. Malarkey said you didn't want to be at the top of the pyramid and suggested I do it instead. That was really nice of you Bren. I know you're not really scared to be up there."

Bren nodded. "I—I just felt bad," she said. "I wasn't trying to take it from you. Honest."

"I know that. I'm sorry I thought so," Suzanne replied. "It's just that I wanted this so bad. You don't *know* how bad. I'll be by for you at five, okay?"

Suzanne turned into the Mickler driveway behind the wheel of her mother's Toyota Tercel at five sharp. Bren ran out the door and was waiting in the grass next to the concrete by the time Suzanne came to a stop.

All the way to school they talked like nothing had ever happened. Bren's spirits soared like a kite catching the first gust of March wind. It was going to be a great night—she could feel it. And when it was over, she'd think of some way to fix things for Jamie, even if it meant going to see the Art Czar herself. For now though, the only thing that mattered was Tad.

Suzanne pulled into the school parking lot and turned off the ignition. Bren opened the passenger door and got out, looking up at the overcast sky. She was just about to say that she hoped it wouldn't rain when she saw it—Tad's candy apple red Thunderbird.

The stars were lined up like a precision marching band, she thought. Tonight was her night! Bren smiled to herself and grabbed her duffel bag.

chapter.12

A light drizzle ushered in the start of the game. Bren shivered in her cotton sweater and pleated skirt, praying it wouldn't rain any harder. She hadn't brought a dryer, and a downpour would make her hair look like sealskin.

Over the loudspeaker system, the hearty voice of the announcer introduced the visiting players. "Starting for Lakeland tonight is nummmmmber fourty-seven, Taaaaaaaaaad Campbell!"

"Go Tad!" Bren yelled and did a cartwheel.

"Are you out of your mind?" Jen Parenti hissed when Bren landed on her feet. "He's from Lakeland, you idiot."

Bren looked out at the crowd. At the front of the stands, a whole row of guys from school booed.

"Sorry. I—I know him, and I just forgot," she muttered, doing another cartwheel to hide her embarrassment.

Suzanne gave her an odd look, but Bren didn't have time to figure out what it meant. The first Edgewood player had crashed through the paper banner held by two girls from the squad. Bren had to run to take her place in the double column of cheerleaders flanking the team as it burst onto the field.

From the start, Edgewood fumbled. By halftime, it looked like the team might as well pack up its pigskin and slink into the locker room.

"We have to really put on a good show for our guys," Ms. Malarkey told the girls before the show. "They can't afford to lose morale at this point. I want you to give it all you've got. But be careful—it's a little slippery on the field. If you think you can't pull something off, improvise."

Bren pranced out onto the field shaking her pompons. She had no idea whether the teams were lined up watching or waiting inside the locker room, but either way she intended to crank up the energy. If Tad saw her in the limelight, he wouldn't be able to resist her sparkle.

"Ready? Okay!" shouted the head cheerleader as they lined up to begin the next cheer.

The Edgewood squad moved like one person, every girl hitting her mark perfectly. The field was slick with mud, but they had encountered the same conditions at practice earlier. Confidence charged the air like static electricity.

"We're going for it!" the head cheerleader announced at the finale. "Everybody okay with the pyramid?"

"Yesssssss!" the entire squad yelled back.

Bren crouched low and placed her hands firmly on the wet ground to make a solid base for the second tier of girls to climb up. When they were in place, Suzanne hopped up first one level and then the next.

Bren tensed as she waited for Suzanne to stand up. After everything that had happened, she truly wanted Suzanne to shine tonight. The girl on top had to extend one arm over her head and the other to the side and kick out her left leg while balancing on her right.

Bren could feel a slight wobble as Suzanne posed, but the roar of the crowd told her she had done it. Relief flooded her until, out of the corner of her eye, she spotted Tad.

"Tad!" Before she knew she'd formed it, the word rushed out of Bren's mouth. She lifted one hand off the ground to wave and tried to stand up. Suddenly arms and legs were everywhere. Tangled. Flailing. Covered in mud. Girls screamed. The crowd soared from hushed shock to deafening laughter.

It had all taken only a nanosecond. Stunned, Bren picked herself up off the ground and looked down at her uniform in horror. She looked like a mud wrester. "Anybody hurt?" the head cheerleader called.

Assured that there were no casualties, she led her rag-tag squad off the field. But not before she glared daggers at Bren.

"I am not even going to ask what you thought you were

doing," Ms. Malarkey barked as Bren passed her. "You're benched, Mickler."

Bren's face blazed hot enough to fry an egg. She slumped onto the bench by the edge of the field and blinked back tears as she watched Lakeland's cheerleaders cartwheel onto the field.

They went from one fantastic routine to the next and ended with two girls standing on the palms of two male cheerleaders' hands. One of them was the redhead from the fair. The redhead tossed her impossible mane of hair and sent the audience a dazzling smile. Bren's mouth dropped open as the redhead bounced off the field, straight into the waiting arms of Tad Campbell. He lifted her up off her feet and swung her around.

"Isn't that sweet?" Suzanne said to Jen Parenti. She pointed at Tad and the redhead, glanced at Bren, and smirked. "They've been going together for two years."

Suzanne knew! Bren realized it with the force of a punch to the stomach. Not only had Suzanne gotten the picture that Bren had a crush on Tad the size of the Grand Canyon, but worse yet, she remembered that Bren had called him her new boyfriend that night at practice.

By the time the game was over, and Edgewood had crawled off the field in disgrace, Bren wanted nothing more than to go home and hide under her bed. She was humiliated. She was stunned. She was hurt to the roots of her soul.

"Hey, you okay?" Maya asked. She wrapped her arms around

Bren and gave her a hug. "Come on—let's get out of here. You can go back to my house and get a shower, and we'll go to the Gnosh. Baby, you need some comfort food."

Bren allowed herself to be led to the parking lot. She didn't even bother going back into the school to collect her stuff. It could wait until Monday. She let Maya open the door of Mr. Beep and gently steer her toward the passenger seat.

"Hey Bren!" a voice called.

Bren looked across the lot. Tad grinned, pointed at his car, and gave her two thumbs up. "Thanks Stargazer!" he hollered, slinging an arm casually around the redhead's shoulders.

"Yeah, thanks!" the redhead echoed.

Bren collapsed her sore body into Maya's car and didn't say a word all the way to the Cross house. Once there, she gratefully headed for the shower and turned on the water as hot as she could stand it. The sharp needles of spray couldn't wash away the night's misery, but she stood under them until the water turned cold enough to make her teeth chatter.

Bren toweled herself off, pulled on a borrowed outfit of Maya's, and opened the bathroom door. Maya's and her mother's voices floated out of the room next door.

"It's too bad Jamie made the decision she did," Dr. Cross said. Her voice sounded like a slightly older Maya. "Garrett Lindstrom spoke to the art faculty and told me himself that she was one of the most gifted students in his seminar. In fact, he mentioned there would be reps coming in from prestigious art schools. Jamie might have gotten a scholarship to one of those summer programs she's been so interested in. He was sure she'd get one. It's just such a shame."

"Wow, that's for sure. What a bad choice!" Maya agreed. "Poor Jamie."

Bren froze in the hallway. She knew a lot about bad choices. She was the *Queen* of Bad Choices. Not only had she gone to cheerleading camp and failed to make head cheerleader, but it had also cost her a special high school internship at one of the major New York fashion houses.

"I couldn't believe you dropped out of the workshop, Bren," the director of the art museum had told her later. "The DKNY people raved over your work. They thought you showed the most promise of all our applicants. And now another girl is in New York City in your place."

Standing in Maya's hallway, Bren felt the sickness of that day at the museum wash over her in a wave. It was too late for her— that was certain. But maybe there was still some way to help Jamie. And salvage this rotten night.

chapter.13

"There's our Bren, looking like her pretty self again!" Dr. Cross said, smiling as Bren came to the open door of Maya's room. "Listen, do you girls mind if I ride along with you to the Gnosh and come home with Dad? He wanted to put something new on the menu tonight and left the bag of goodies here in the pantry."

"Fine by me," Bren replied. "We better go though. It's getting late. I really held things up."

Maya jumped off the bed and grabbed her car keys. "Ready when you guys are!" she said. "Come on Mom, let's hit it!"

Dr. Cross led the way downstairs, shrugged into her coat, and grabbed a brown paper bag out of the pantry on her way out the door. Bren squeezed into the tiny backseat of Mr. Beep and let Dr. Cross take the front passenger seat. All the way to the Gnosh, Maya and her mom chatted about the disastrous game while Bren brooded over what to say to Jamie.

The Gnosh was surprisingly quiet for a Friday night. Dr. Cross opened the door and went in first. A whiny old 50s love song poured mournfully out of the jukebox.

"Hi girls!" Dr. Cross greeted the TodayGirls scattered around the dining room. "I'm going back to the kitchen," she informed Maya and Bren. "You two have fun."

For a second Bren and Maya stood by the door taking in the bleak scene. Amber sat alone in a booth against the wall sipping a Diet Sprite and leafing through a magazine. She'd looked up long enough to wave at Dr. Cross, but refused to acknowledge the girls' presence. Morgan and Alex shared a table in the center of the room. The look on Alex's face was so anguished it would wring tears out of the Grinch.

"Oooh-weee!" Maya said softly. "Our girl Alex is not a happy camper tonight."

"Who is?" Bren muttered. She looked around for Jamie and found her stacking plates near the salad bar. "I'm going to go talk to Jamie. I'll be right back."

Bren walked over to the salad bar, praying for the right words.

"Hi," she said at Jamie's elbow. "Can you take a break? I need to talk to you."

"Sure," Jamie agreed. "Just let me finish up here." She set down an armload of plates, wiped up a creamy Italian dressing spill, and led the way to a booth. "What's up? You look a little freaked. What's wrong?"

Bren slid into the booth and groaned. "I wouldn't know where to start," she admitted. "Let's just say that I may never be able to show my face in school again. But that's not the thing that's really bugging me. It's you, Jamie."

"Me?" Jamie looked surprised.

"Yes, you. Everything's a mess. Amber's mad. Maya got hurt. Alex is sad. And you made a bad choice about the art class—thanks to me."

Jamie shook her head. "Don't blame yourself," she said softly. "I'm the one who made the final decision."

"Well then you have to unmake it!" Bren leaned across the table and grabbed both of Jamie's hands. "Listen to me! This summer I did something stupid and lost an internship in New York."

Jamie's eyes widened. "Huh? You never said anything about any internship! When was this?"

Bren gave Jamie's hands a squeeze and released them. "Back in June when I went to cheerleading camp and dropped out of the DKNY deal at the museum. I thought I was going to make head cheerleader and I didn't. And then I found out I was the one who was supposed to get the internship. That's why I've been scared to death to make decisions all summer. I lost faith in my ability to do it."

She looked down at the tabletop, swallowed hard, and looked back up at her friend. "Don't be stupid like I was, Jamie. Please don't! I heard Dr. Cross say that Garrett Lindstrom thinks you're the best one in the class. He also said there are going to be art reps coming from those summer programs you want to go to. You have to get back in that seminar somehow!"

Jamie shook her head sadly. "Garrett Lindstrom never said that," she replied. "No way! I told you he hates me and hates my work even more. I can't go groveling back at this point. It's over. We both made mistakes. All we can do is try to do better next time." Jamie slid out of the booth. "I have to get back to work," she said.

Bren watched her disappear through the swinging door to the kitchen and fought the urge to run after her, knock her to the floor, and sit on her until she listened. I'll just have to go see Garrett Lindstrom myself, she decided.

One way or the other Jamie was getting back in that class. She looked up as the restaurant door opened and Jared came in. Morgan jumped up from her table so fast she almost knocked over her chair. "Jared!" she called running over to him. "There you are! You want to go over to the dance or stay here?"

Bren's mouth dropped open as Jared checked his watch, then looked at Morgan like she was the Invisible Girl. "Neither. I'm—uh—meeting someone," he said.

"Meeting someone? Who?" Morgan asked.

"Uh—a girl. A Sagittarius I met in study hall." He looked over at Bren.

"But . . . but . . . I don't understand," Morgan stuttered. "We always go to stuff *together*. Why are you acting like this, Jared?" Even from the booth, Bren could see Morgan's dark eyes filling up with tears.

Jared shrugged and walked over to the window to look for his date. Morgan ran past Bren into the ladies' room, banging the door behind her.

For a split second, Bren was too stunned to react. Nice Guy Jared had morphed into a Bad Boy the first week of high school! She stood up and stormed over to him. "What do you think you're doing?" she demanded. "You made Morgan cry, and you don't even care."

"You're the one who told me to stay away from Scorpios," he muttered, casually unzipping his jacket.

Bren stared at him like he'd just stepped out of a flying saucer accompanied by a pack of little green guys. She didn't even know this nasty, cold, uncaring person standing in front of her. She turned around and locked gazes with Alex who looked on the verge of tears herself.

"Alex, what's the matter?" Bren dropped into Morgan's empty chair. "Tell me—what's wrong?"

"My mother isn't coming this week," Alex replied with no trace of her usual bravado. "And she's not coming later either. She had the money, and now she doesn't. Part of the roof was damaged in the tornado, and it'll cost a fortune to fix it."

Bren's mind spun like a tornado. So much calamity at once

was like being struck head-on by a train traveling at the speed of light. She looked at Alex's sorrowful face, at Amber sitting alone, at Jared by the window, at Maya sitting at the table next to Alex with her bandage poking out from under her sweater, and at the two doors that had swallowed up Morgan and Jamie. She jumped to her feet.

"Listen, you guys. Everybody, please—listen!" she cried. She knew there were people in the restaurant who must be thinking that she'd rattled her brains in the fall on the football field, but she didn't care. The whole world had gone topsy-turvy all because she was stupid enough to think you could tell the future by the stars.

"I'm sorry I ever got into this whole fortune-telling mess. It was stupid, and now it's caused all this trouble and I don't know what to do to make it right and—" Tears sprang to her eyes, forcing her to stop and regain her composure. In the background, the whiny singer begged somebody to tell Laura that he loved her.

The door to the kitchen sprang open, and Jamie and Dr. Cross emerged, each carrying a small tray.

"Hey everybody! Mr. Cross wants to try out the latest addition to the menu," Jamie announced. "Free fortune cookies for everyone!"

Bren gaped at Jamie. Fortune cookies! Was Jamie crazy? Had Mr. Cross slipped on some grease in the kitchen and fallen on his head? The last thing in the world anybody at the Gnosh needed at this moment was fortune cookies.

Jamie ignored Bren and went around the room passing the tray. Everyone, including Amber, took a cellophane wrapped cookie. Amber tore the wrapping off hers with her teeth, cracked open the cookie, and read the slip of paper inside. Then she stood up and came over to stand by the group clustered at Maya and Alex's table.

The door of the ladies' room opened, and Morgan came out, took a cookie, and cracked hers open too. One by one, everyone, including Jared, took a cookie, opened it, and read the slip of paper tucked inside. The entire scene was played out in almost total silence. The only sound came from the jukebox, which had switched to a song about a girl named Patches who'd drowned in the river.

Bren was the only one who had not reached for a cookie.

"Let me read mine," Amber said, breaking the weird silence. She cleared her throat and read, "'Your word is like a lamp for my feet and a light for my way.—Psalm 119:105'"

It was the very first Thought for the Day Amber had ever posted. Bren stared in astonishment. How could . . .

"I'm next," Maya said. She unfolded the small scrap of white paper and read, "'God is our God forever and ever. He will guide us from now on.—Psalm 48:14'"

Around the circle they went, each person reading a different verse. When they were finished Bren felt as though a circle of sparrows were tweeting around her head. It was all so impossible.

And yet at the same time, there was a rightness about it that made her want to laugh and cry at the same time.

"I don't see how . . ." she began.

"Take a cookie," Dr. Cross interrupted. She presented Bren with her tray. One lonely cookie sat all by itself on a paper doily.

Bren took the cookie, conscious of seven pairs of eyes watching her. Slowly, she cracked it open and pulled out the slip of paper inside.

"Read it!" Maya ordered.

"'Your friends have taught you a lesson,'" Bren read. "'GOTCHA!'" She stared at the circle in astonishment. "You mean this was all a setup?" she demanded.

Maya whipped off her bandage in reply. Morgan and Jared linked arms. Alex, Jamie, and Dr. Cross laughed so hard they had to hang onto each other.

"You mean you aren't hurt?" Bren asked Maya.

"Nope," Maya said, snapping her wrist back and forth.

"And we're still best buds," Morgan offered, playfully cuffing Jared on the chin with her free hand.

"I don't have a date with any Sagittarius," he added.

"My mom wasn't really coming to Edgewood," Alex put in.

"And I never really quit the seminar," Jamie added.

Bren could hardly take it in. Before she could reply, Jason Hersh came through the door, shaking rain off his navy blue windbreaker. He took one look at the group standing in the middle of the room and stopped, his face turning redder than Tad's Thunderbird. Bren laughed with relief and ran over to him.

"It's okay," she assured him. "I already know. You don't have to play along. The joke's out."

"Huh? What joke? I don't . . ."

Bren looked at Jason's bewildered face, then at the group, then back at Jason. "You mean you're not in on it? I thought you were and that you'd come to . . ."

Before she could say "take me to the dance after all," the door opened again and Suzanne Kennedy breezed through. She saw Bren standing by Jason and frowned. "Jas, are you ready to go?" she asked, glaring at Bren.

"Sure am," Jason replied. He took Suzanne's hand and drew her to the door. "Uh—bye Bren, bye everybody," he muttered.

Bren stood for a moment staring after them. Jason and Suzanne had a date! They were a couple. He hadn't wasted one day crying over Bren Mickler. He had a new girlfriend and from the looks of things, she was crazy about him. Slowly, Bren turned back to the group. "I think maybe I deserved that, huh?" she said in a small voice.

"I'm sorry, babe, but you did," Maya said, laughing. "Suzanne Kennedy has had a crush on that dude since last year. Why do you think she wanted to be on top of the pyramid so bad? She wanted him to notice her!"

Bren pulled a chair from an adjoining table and sank into

it. This, she decided, had to have been the weirdest day of her life.

"So you were all in on it," she said when she could talk. "Everybody except Amber, right?"

Seven pairs of eyes exchanged glances. For a second nobody said a word. And then Amber burst out laughing, her blue eyes dancing with delight. "Oh, I wouldn't be so sure about *that!*" she said. "Who do you think made the cookies?"

Epilogue

The next morning Bren slept until noon. When she finally crawled out of bed and logged on to her computer, the usual Saturday morning chat was already in full wing. She scanned the girls' conversation:

nycbutterfly: guess we got HER good, huh?

faithful1: could hardly handle it--was so funny

TX2step: I nearly lost it when she asked me what was wrong. LOL!!!

rembrandt: I don't know about U, but I felt sort of sorry 4 her. Especially when she was begging me 2 get back in the seminar.

jellybean: I'm with rembrandt. I felt sorry 4 her 2.

nycbutterfly: me 2. How could u not? Poor girl got hit from every direction. but U gotta admit--we were good actors!
TX2step: we were so good we were bad!

Bren jumped right in the middle:

chicChick: u think so? well, let me give U some advice from the stars--and not the ones in the sky either! I've had enough of those 4ever!
nycbutterfly: what advice is that?
chicChick: Don't buy dresses for the Oscars!
nycbutterfly: Whaaaaaat? U saying we can't act?
TX2step: Ack! That is so not true!
faithful1: yeah, where do U get that?

Bren chuckled. Pretty soon they'd be auditioning for the school play just to prove her wrong. She hit the caps lock button and typed with satisfaction:

ChicChick: FORTUNE FAIRY SAYS GOTCHA!

Net Ready, Set, Go!

I hope my words and thoughts please you.
Psalm 19:14

The characters of TodaysGirls.com chat online in the safest—and maybe most fun—of all chat rooms! They've created their own private Web site and room! Many Christian teen sites allow you to create your own private chat rooms, and there are other safe options.

Work with your parents to develop a list of safe, appropriate chat rooms. Earn Internet freedom by showing them you can make the right choices. *Honor your father and your mother (Deuteronomy 5:16).*

Before entering a chat room, you'll select a user name. Although you can use your real name, a nickname is safer. Most people choose one that says something about who they are, like Amber's name, faithful1. Don't be discouraged if the name you select is already taken. You can use a similar one by adding a number at its end.

No one will notice your grammar in a chat room. Don't worry if you spell something wrong or forget to capitalize. Some people even misspell words on purpose. You might see a sentence like How R U?

But sometimes it's important to be accurate. Web site and e-mail addresses must be exact. Pay close attention to whether letters are upper- or lowercase. Remember that Web site addresses don't use some punctuation marks, such as hyphens and apostrophes. (That's why the "Today's" in TodaysGirls.com has no apostrophe!) And instead of spaces between words, underlines are often used to_make_a_space. And sometimes words just run together like onebigword.

When you're in a chat room, remember real people are typing the words that appear on your screen. Treat them with the same respect you expect from them. Don't say anything you wouldn't want repeated in Sunday school. *Do for other people what you want them to do for you (Luke 6:31).*

Sometimes people say mean, hurtful things—things that make us angry. This can happen in chat rooms, too. In some chat rooms, you can highlight a rude person's name and click a button that says, "ignore," which will make his or her comments disappear from your screen. You always have the option to switch rooms or sign off. If a particular person becomes a continual problem, or if someone says something especially vicious, you should report this problem user to the chat service. *Ask God to bless those who say bad things to you. Pray for those who are cruel (Luke 6:28–29).*

Remember that Internet information is not always factual. Whether you're chatting or surfing Web sites, be skeptical about information and people. Not everything on the Internet is true. You don't have to be afraid of the Internet, but you should always be cautious. Practice caution with others even in Christian chat rooms.

It's OK to chat about your likes and dislikes, but *never* give out personal information. Do not tell anyone your name, phone number, address, or even the name of your school, team, church, or neighborhood. Be cautious. . . . *You will be like sheep among wolves. So be as smart as snakes. But also be like doves and do nothing wrong. Be careful of people (Matthew 10:16–17).*

N 2 DEEP & STRANGER ONLINE

AMBER THOMAS

16/junior
e-name: faithful1
best friend: Maya
site area: Thought for the Day

Confident. Caring. Swimmer. Single-handedly built TodaysGirls.com Web site. Loves her folks. Big brother Ryan drives her nuts! Great friend. Got a problem? Go to Amber.

JAMIE CHANDLER

PLEASE REPLY! & PORTRAIT OF LIES

15/sophomore
e-name: rembrandt
best friend: Bren
site area: Artist's Corner

Quiet. Talented artist. Works at the Gnosh Pit after school. Dad left when she was little. Helps her mom with younger sisters Jordan and Jessica. Baby-sits for Coach Short's kids.

ALEX DIAZ

4GIVE & 4GET & TANGLED WEB

14/freshman
e-name: TX2step
best friend: Morgan
site area: Entertain Us

Spicy. Hot-tempered Texan. Lives with grandparents because of parents' problems. Won state in freestyle swimming at her old school. Snoops. Into everything. Breaks the rules.

POWER DRIVE & R U 4 REAL?
16/junior
e-name: nycbutterfly
best friend: Amber
site area: What's Hot—What's Not

MAYA CROSS

Fashion freak. Health nut. Grew up in New York City.
Small town drives her crazy. Loves to dance.
Dad owns the Gnosh Pit. Little sis Morgan is also
a TodaysGirl.

BREN MICKLER

UNPREDICTABLE & LUV@FIRST SITE
15/sophomore
e-name: chicChick
best friend: Jamie
site area: Smashin' Fashion

Funny. Popular. Outgoing. Spaz. Cheerleader.
Always late. Only child. Wealthy family. Bren is
chatting—about anything, online and off—
except when she's eating junk food.

UN E-FARM & CHAT FREAK
4/freshman
e-name: jellybean
est friend: Alex
ite area: Feeling All Write

MORGAN
CROSS

he Web-ster. Spends too much time online. Overalls.
1&Ms. Swim team. Tries to save the world. Close to her
amily—when her big sister isn't bossing her around.

Cyber Glossary

Bounced mail An e-mail that has been returned to its sender.

Chat A live conversation—typed or spoken through microphones—among individuals in a chat room.

Chat room A "place" on the Internet where individuals meet to "talk" with one another.

Crack To break a security code.

Download To receive information from a more powerful computer.

E-mail Electronic mail sent through the Internet.

E-mail address An Internet address where e-mail is received.

File Any document or image stored on a computer.

Floppy disk A small, thin plastic object that stores information to be accessed by a computer.

Hacker Someone who tries to gain unauthorized access to another computer or network of computers.

Header Text at the beginning of an e-mail that identifies the sender, subject matter, and the time at which it was sent.

Home page A Web site's first page.

Internet A worldwide electronic network that connects computers to each other.

Link Highlighted text or a graphic element that may be clicked with the mouse in order to "surf" to another Web site or page.

Log on/Log in To connect to a computer network.

Modem A device that enables computers to exchange information.

The Net The Internet.

Newbie A person who is learning or participating in something new.

Online To have Internet access. Can also mean to use the Internet.

Surf To move from page to page through links on the Web.

Upload To send information to a more powerful computer.

The Web The World Wide Web or WWW.